MW01135931

R. READ

This is a work of fiction. Names, characters, businesses, places, events and incidents are described herein as a product of the author's imagination. Any resemblance to actual persons, living or dead, or actual events is purely fictional. Some names and identifying details have been added or altered to protect the privacy of individuals who may see some truth herein.

The story being told is meant to supplement student athlete orientation materials distributed at Universities worldwide. If you would like to respond, or reach the author with comments, please email shetoobook@gmail.com with your inquiry.

Copyright © 2017 R. Read. All rights reserved. This book or any portion thereof may not be reproduced or used in any manner whatsoever without the express written permission of the author except for the use of brief quotations in a book review.

For permission requests contact:

shetoobook@gmail.com

Attention: R. Read

CONTENTS

INTRODUCTION

Thursday September 22 - off campus.

Crime log stated the victim was intoxicated and the rape included sodomy and oral copulation. Campus Criminal Investigation Bureau (CCIB) is investigating the crime, according to a campus alert sent Friday.

This is not the first reported sexual assault the CCIB has responded to at a campus residential hall this year, month or week. Things are always hopping in those first few weeks as new students arrive on campus.

September 14, campus police detained a suspect on suspicion of raping a 19-year-old female student in campus housing September 4; ten days after the incident had occurred. Should we believe her? Can she prove it? Does that matter to anyone?

Additionally, campus police responded to three sexual

assaults that might have occurred during a concert at the Greek Theater on September 10. Does that matter?

Should we be concerned? Is this officially now *the fabric of our lives*? In our story today, Frankie and Beau are off campus. When the incident occurs Thursday, September 22 off campus, it is not a University affair or is it?

PART I

Headline: Alumni Weekend Get Your Tickets and Tailgates Set

Tickets still on sale for Friday pre-game party on the patio level at stadium. Game day good seats still available but going fast. Special Guest TBA. First 1300 in gate free bobble heads.

@BB: fuck the football game, join us at AKE for FOAM PARTY SATURDAY. #fffoam

@PM: buck the ducks, get in on the action at the Barge tnite. #longlivethebarge

@MRD: we gonna blow them ducks outta the watah. #calfootballforlife

Little Black Dress Night

For as long as Frankie could remember, she had participated in an annual ritual of three to four weeks of hot summer sports practices known as *pre-season*.

Most fall scholar athletes gathered before the rest of their classmates, in mid to late August, for exhausting workouts, countless hours of team bonding, game planning, tee shirt creating, and parties of some sort.

She'd cleverly switched to curling in grade 10 when she read an article published in the local paper about the probability of being awarded college scholarship dollars for this relatively random sport. Also key was that hardly anyone who went out for it got cut. As she set out on a concerted effort to fund her dream of ditching her Texas roots for the great state of California, curling would be her ticket. Partially the scholarship dollars, somewhat the easier training and conditioning involved, but mostly the guarantee of a college experience outside of Texas.

Sure there was plenty of cardio, weights, conditioning, and on-ice practice time, but nothing compared to soccer. Frankie did not miss the soccer grind of practicing twice per day during those weeks before the school, usually in hot summer temperatures, only to be outrun by an underclassperson in the final tryout. Soccer presented much more grueling workouts, followed by pre-season scrimmages in heat, while curling was downright pleasant in comparison, indoors and chilly.

4

Aside from lunges, interval conditioning and weight training, curling teams basically just held inter-squad matches. There were barely enough curlers to field three squads of foursomes for a top, middle, or backup squads. With so few interested in the sport, you were practically guaranteed a spot. Add Frankie's bit of athleticism, she was coveted by the coach.

Frankie could tell by the first week of practice which girls had followed the take home conditioning planners, and who likely partied away their summer nights, making out, smoking pot and drinking. It was almost too easy to do about half the expected work, party part-time, and still be good to go on the ice with her athleticism by tryout time.

At the college level, pre-season hype and mania was amplified by the mixing of student athletes from foreign countries and multiple states. Let the groups loose on campus a solid month prior to the academic only student body, and some wild parties ensued.

Traditionally, curlers let off a bit of steam after pre-season and tryouts for squads with a little black dress night party. Nothing athletic about it, a night out as collegiate girly girls, a highpoint with celebrated stories from years past. Being a red-shirt sophomore, Frankie was an experienced party leader, hosting the pregame before heading out to a campus fraternity party.

The squads giggle as they twirl each other's hair into loose, cascading curls and waves. Straightened, then curled, it's all the rage on the latest blow out bar menu.

5

"Oh my gawd Marla. You are truly an ahrteest – that updo on this betch is straight up glam!" Beth holds out a shot of tequila to Frankie while holding back the lime.

"Ima keep it real wit chu sistahs; Beau is mine tonight," Frankie gulps the liquid then grips the lime with her front teeth to suck out the chaser. "Audrey fuckin Hepburn's got nothin' on me."

"I know you be talkin' Breakfast at Tiff, Beau's place gurl." Beth and a few others laugh as if it's comedy central ready material.

Incoming freshmen are the stylists to the upper-class, as is part of the historic ritual of Cal Curling Crew. Marla is a transfer with mad braiding skills. Make-up is strewn across the desks and dining room table where ten or more gather for a group get up and go.

Jane makes her way from the kitchen to the back bedroom with a paper plate loaded with eight shot glasses filled to the brim. "Who's up?!"

"Bottoms up ladies," Beth and Anne clink their shots. "Wimps and bed wetter's need not apply."

A couple girls sip timidly and Jane scolds "get on our level betches, drop it back."

"Seriously tequila shots is appetizer. Be ready for your main course drinks." Anne adds. "Curlers never say no to free alcohol."

Hazing is so last year. Drinking to oblivion is simply PreGaming. No worries.

There is frenzy in the kitchen area while dozens of limes are sliced. Coarse salt and special sugar-rimmed glasses are also being prepped. The freshmen have been ICED with a Smirnoff each, but upper-class chicks stick to straight vodka to save calories.

A pair of four-inch heels might seem like a bit of a challenge for trekking across campus, but again, no worries, liquid courage/pain relief on board. Dresses are tried and traded. Spanx encased bodies are flitting about, and "does this romper make me look fat?"

How is it these twenty-somethings don't realize their bodies are perfect as is...and this is as good as it gets in terms of the figures they've been given. *Born this Way*, everybody knows that one. Not since thong swimsuits became mainstream has there been more body shaming.

"Circle up betches, time to rave it out. Jane cue me some Salt N Pepa," Frankie orders. "Let's talk about sex lay dees," she chants her version of the lyrics, taking lead on hip sway and grinding against the arm of the couch. The rest of the group join in on a groove session.

The party is being thrown by the Boy Boaters. Hunky, tall and strong are they...especially after a few drinks. So what if their reputation is shhhitt. The parties are always off the chain. Let's Goooooooo.

Frankie is a junior. Older. Wiser. There are four in her UberX. She orders it a block off College Ave, and they jump out a block from the party. No one needs to spill the beans. Feet saved.

"Drop us a block from the barge," orders Frankie to the Uber driver.

"Huh?" Uber driver.

"Oh wait, just kidding. We are headed to a party at the Boat House. They call it the barge. Corner of Piedmont and Bancroft."

"Wait. A block from there, k?" Frankie quickly corrects her error. It needs to look like they all walked or the team will mock 'em.

It's less than a mile and the Uber driver is annoyed. *These damn sorority bitches never tip and fucking slowing my ass down tonight...I gotta get off college row already.* $6.45 is the total on his screen as he begrudgingly smiles, knowing full well just one of these four bitches gives him a bad rating and his tips of the future are nil.

"Anne and Beth, buddy system. Jane, you're with me. There's a guy I want you to meet." Just like that the four become two twos, and they're off.

Boaters Night

For the most part, Boaters at Cal need no introduction. Oarsman for the Golden Bears are Olympic legends, successful businessmen, and proudly Cal's oldest organized sport. Dozens of gold medals, time-honored traditions. It's earned its reputation as the eldest and most successful sport against rival Stanford, year after year for those of you uninformed.

Needless to say, successful with the ladies. Since the late 1800's boating at Cal—having been started by a group of students—has truly become one of their grandest sports, certainly in the minds of the boaters.

Ask anyone who's tried it, boating is a sport where even the sturdiest of athletes routinely faint as they cross finish lines, having given it their all physically and mentally. A most grueling sport, for only the toughest of men; character, strength, and stamina combined. Never give up; agony is expected; you believe yourself to be nearing death's door during those last half miles. Legacy boaters understand what is expected of them having heard fathers of fathers describe their most memorable pulls.

Beauregard Pierce—aka Beau, and Bryce Howard—aka Dewey, have been rowing boats together since childhood near Lake Nacimiento in Central California. Dexter and Chandoon, being too small of communities to have their own teams, the two boys found each other skipping rocks avoiding the hot sun—and the workout—one sunny summer camp day.

Both boys in middle school were sinewy and strong. High school chubs would surely convert to muscle once the collegiate level work-outs took them to next level boating competitions.

Dewey is a legacy man. His father and grandfather both have medals and photos hanging loud and proud in their respective man caves. Grandpa has an Olympic Gold. Dewey likes to *wear gold*, but expectations are lowered as he has neither the build nor the drive of a champion. Mom always says, *'more of me to love'* when, in fact, he is clearly nearing obesity.

Beau has worked for it. He has worked hard every day knowing the only way out of this shithole town was through a D1 scholarship in boating. His father left when he was too young to remember it. Single motherhood life was living on the 'less than' side of the tracks.

Dewey has his father's credit card, the one that Dad's secretary *swears* he *never* even reviews, so he is lead on party shopping.

Vodka is cheap. Fireball, cheaper and has a handle.

"Dude. Grab a lemonade or some shit, it needs to taste fruity." His formula for Jungle Juice never really required a recipe aside from that. "Get three gallons."

Freshmen back at the house are "cleaning". For the most part, this constitutes pushing all the furniture against the walls to open up the dance floor. This also serves as sweeping being that the dust bunnies slide on outwards to the corners of the room.

The gang is going to need a bigger dance floor tonight. It's fall scavenger hunt night. Rival campus Greeks send crews over to brother/sister houses for a bit of search and savagery.

Boaters hold the record from years back having rope hooked twenty-nine pairs of Stanford panties that stretched across the ballroom rafters end to end; nearly forty feet. Lesser hauls were lovely banister garland or drapery garnish throughout the place. It'd be tough to ever beat that record these days...so few dames in any panties at all.

Most of the upper classmen are out back on the black top for some hoops.

"Beau. You line up a team for us tonight? And not those softball dykes. We need fresh meat. Heard the curling team has foreigners. Those dames put out."

"Hell yes. The French know how it's done," chimes John, from the half parking lot mark.

John Laskey is a legacy man. Six-foot-three with thick dark brown hair; he has no trouble gettin' with the ladies.

Blake Laskey, his father, was big man on campus way back when, proud as hell that the prodigal son made the squad two years ago. *Pops'll be pulling' in on Saturday for the big alumni game and tailgate; maybe I'll have a fine piece of foreign ass to show off.*

11

"Yup. Frankie promised to bring the freshies, two Germans and a Belgian, I think. Not sure if the Aussie is on campus yet, but I call shotgun if she shows."

Beau is his most confident self. Getting into Cal was heroic at the high school level, but this shit was lit. Just the word BOATER on his sleeve was enough to get even the hottest bods on board for a good solid rub and tug.

Beau took a moment to laugh out loud, thinking about how nervous he was just three short years ago. Dating a "good catholic girl" for most of his four high school years, he had been unsure about college life and sexual performance.

Absolutely no one could know he was a virgin headed to campus. Orientation was enough stress—freshman Boat Week he'd be challenged for sure. Stories floated all up and down his pack of pals who'd heard from friends of friends. Blow jobs, gang bangs; sex, more sex, and *anal sex*. Millennials are free spirits for sure—hippies got nothing on them—friends with benefits, swipe right, Bumble booty calls baby. Forget *"shoving a burger down her throat"* like Andrew Dice Clay always used to say, just *smack her around a bit* 'til she begs for it.

Turns out he'd worried for nada. Most of the time you either got a decent blow job on site or your take home was so out of it *she asked him if she was good*.

Easy enough, "best ever baby," he'd assure his shes. Forget to bring a condom? No problem. Turn your back to her, spit out your gum and stretch it across the tip, *badda boom badda bang*. Drunk bitches don't nitpick.

That first semester he'd learned his lesson about too much oral and the chafing. Alcohol, in fact, dries out the foreskin so be sure to offer up a piece of candy or some gummy bears before you *send her downtown*. Edible lubricant costs dough. Any saliva-driving hard candy will usually do the trick.

Never ever let her go down without a little something. Funny side note, coconut oil is all the rage these days... babes put it in their hair or some shit, so you can almost always find a little oily edible in the pantry.

Tonight's party on the barge would be a slam dunk. Frankie was primed and ready—he'd felt it full on during their "coffee date" on Thursday.

On campus, public intoxication was a bit of a worry. Coffee shops were keen for Wi-Fi and hot cups; in all shapes and sizes those cups. Who needs liquor these days when getting a hand job under the table was for sugar in your tea, if you were a student athlete.

Sit close enough to her, order black coffee or tea and let the creaming begin.

Less than 30 seconds of wrangling the panties and fingering a bit of honey. He always brought his hand up from below and immediately dipped his finger right into his cup. Squeals of pleasure, often times followed by a jump onto his lap right there in the café, then the pleading. "Take me back to your place for a little afternoon delight, Beau."

Wonder if that Aussie is blonde or brunette. Ah, who cares, I likes me the freshest. And sticking with Frankie after two or three coffee dates was the wise choice—the sure thing.

"Dude. Are you playing or what? Pass the fucking ball, Beau."

Reporting to campus in early August gave fall student athletes that false sense of "I got this" way earlier than the general population of students. They get a month of quiet on campus to explore the pizza joints and coffee stops with no long lines, merchants enjoying a bit of "time off" from the full student frenzy of fall. Often times, they know their barista and or "pizza man" by end of August, and the monogrammed Dri-Fit becomes a sort of code for "student athlete, serve us well."

You cannot simply say "entitled" about student athletes because many hours of play went into the getting here. So few athletes actually make it to the Division I collegiate level, therefore, a certain amount of time and effort has been exerted by the individual athlete. But it is probably documented somewhere that in order to become an athlete at that level, you had to have had a support system of some sort. Dollars often decreed private lessons and play levels above average. At private schools, as well as at Cal, athletes are frequently on the "haves" side of today's society.

Cal athletes receive free clothing, gear and shoes. They have cleaning service in their dorm rooms. Frequently, they have additional cash from stipend; which for some kids is money they never had at home. At least not in accounts accessible to them aside from asking their parents.

Student athletes at Cal are, more often than not, on the brightest side of the sidewalk most days. All that sun has some of them acting as if they are a cut above.

For the ladies, pre-gaming had started about 7 and it's nearly 10. Having spent nearly three hours doing shots of tequila or cheap vodka, they spritz their team-mates' JLo perfume in all the right places.

When Frankie and the crew arrive at the barge, they are primed and ready.

"Hey Dooooooo eeee. Where's my main squeeze Bow Boy," oozes Frankie.

"Not so fast ma lady. Gimme some sugar," replies Dewey.

Jane giggles with delight as Frankie presses her breasts into the deep belly Dewey acquired after freshman dorm food. He's no longer his high school lean and mean self, but a bulky, thick and meaty has-been boater, with a fair amount of straight up fat around the belly. *'More cushion for the pushing,'* he liked to say.

For half a second Jane wonders to herself if Dewey can even see over that big fat belly to his penis for any action. Another giggle to herself.

"I'm off to catch up to A and B; the sophies are more fun." Jane taps at Frankie's arm then scoots off.

Anne and Beth became A and B on their recruiting visit —'always blasted'—those not privy to the inside joke none the wiser. Anne from Holland, Beth from Germany where 'drinking age' really isn't a thing. Sophomore star curlers, these two were drinking pros from way before Cal. She can see them belly up to the bar from here and she needs just a little red cup to get settled in.

Later, Jane will recant to police, that was the last time she saw Frankie that night.

Having caught up to A and B, the three dip red cups into the punch bin just in case they get thirsty while on the dance floor. It's a standard issue black garbage bin and they have to lean in as the punch is already half gone by now. It's always best to have a drink in your hand when you dance, the liquid back and forth in the cup lets you know you're truly gettin' down.

Frankie has to punch Dewey with both arms to release herself from his grip.

"Come on now, don't play shy," he coos.

Turns out he's taste-tested the punch and the liquor bottles while mixing, release from his grip is none too easy for Frankie.

She feels her shoulders being pulled backwards and lands in the capable arms of Beau. *Thank heavens*. She lets out a deep breath. *My knight in shining Dri Fit.*

The soft and slick feel of the fabric is jaded by the sweat permeated smell of B.O. and a vinegar-like odor she cannot quite place...

I swear these guys do not own clothing other than what they are given by the team. A slight longing for the Izod twill long sleeves and khaki pants boys back home wore. Way back when guys actually made attempts to look good for a girl they were interested in. That thought lasts less than four seconds, when Beau's tongue is jammed in her mouth and immediately hits her molars.

Oh. My. God. Is he trying to hit the gag reflex back there? I just might be sick. Before she can actually throw up, Beau has her airborne, tossed over his shoulder and headed to the porch for some fresh air.

"You look like I need a drink." He laughs, as he plops her onto the shredded brown couch that's weathered more than a few NorCal rain storms. "I'll be right back. Don't move," he instructs her.

17

"Is that an order or can I get some love on the dance floor, Aoki is my jam," she says out loud to no one in particular as *Delirious* blares from the front room. She sings along, "Til the sun up / twisted burnt up / can't nooooo body stop us /gone delirious." Lyrics waft to her ears from the ballroom.

Beau is off to the bar. "May I have this dance," she again is speaking just to herself. "Why of course m'lady. Let's boogie," in her best London dialect.

With that, the memory of the night becomes blurry.

Stanford Ladies

On the other side of the bay, anticipation over the annual scavenger hunt is abuzz as the lady's swim team at Stanford finish their final conditioning laps Thursday and hit the locker room. Much like their rival's little black dress night, enemy campus scavenger hunts were legendary parties you'd hear about from years past, and talk about for years to come.

"You going?"

"Never missed one; fourth and final."

"It's my first. I had pneumonia last year."

"Oh hey. Scavenger Hunt Virgin. Get ready to get lit."

"Virgins fly first. You'll be the captain of your group and lady it is none too easy. Maybe eating a cricket, maybe *swallowing a little something else*." The entire locker room falls into laughter.

"Nord asked me to stay back—can you even imagine— who does he think I am? *His property*? I wouldn't miss it for...well, maybe for...shit no way, not missing it. Even if Brad Pitt says he's going down on me tonight!"

Jessica was a captain last year. It's her chance to get back at the betches who made her eat freaking dirt and Sharpied her face with a dozen or more penises before they ever even headed out. Forget drinking a gallon of milk, these freshies were doing shots. Lots of them.

"I got the short straw. Driver," mumbled Harper. "Jess, you *have* to be in my group. I can't wait to see your Dolce & Gabbana dress tonight."

"Ah yes. Have not secured that just yet, but headed home to dinner with the 'rents and will grab it. Still had the tags on last I checked so we'll have to do some of that 'return tag gun action' on it before I put it back. It's so clutch that Julia worked at GAP last summer and kept the tagging gun."

"Listen betches. I am gonna start charging for that shit. Five dollah make you hollah." Again, laughter among the masses as they dried and strutted out to their respective automobiles; no scooters for these elite athletes.

"Where's pre game?" Harper already behind the wheel, headed to gas up on daddy's credit card and get the Beamer washed.

"Angie's; her folks are out of town."

"Super cool. See you about 9. Wait. Julia, you're doing my hair. Be there by 8."

"Yessim. At your suhvice bella...mahsta bella." Julia's best southern slant on it.

"Hold up. Who's got ID for the BevMo stop?" Harper ever the organizer.

"On it." Jackie holds a gold card and a red and white BevMo membership one high in the air.

"Just Garden Goddess for shots. Keep the Goose in the trunk for us."

"Lemonade or Ginger Beer?" Jackie wants to impress as she's new to the team.

"Both." Harper will make mules for the cool kids, freshies chase with lemonade.

"See ya."

"Ciao Bellas."

"Later Gaters."

"You wanna be me too."

They all zoom outta the lot in separate vehicles, iTunes cued up and blaring.

Angie has dismissed the kitchen and dining staff at her folks' place early in order to get set. Not before they'd prepped bacon wrapped scallops, chicken skewers, and a host of other plated appetizers though. She slipped the head cook a Franklin and smiled pretty at the rest of the household staff.

"Maybe she'll take you all out to Chuck E. Cheese—*hasta luego.*" One of a handful of her Spanish language greetings. Now then. Where did she hide the Casamigos tequila—the gang will love that she got George Clooney's favorite for shots.

Dammit. Why did I let Rosa leave before I remembered the limes? Details, details. *I'll have to cut them myself.*

Harper arrives first. A bit early actually, it's only 7:40.

"Can I borrow a dress? I just got freaking water splashes on me at the fuckin' drive-thru wash. Damn window wasn't all the way up."

The two giggle and trot upstairs to Angie's dressing room. It's a McMansion of sorts and she has a walk-in for her casual clothes separate from her formal wear and shoes nook off the main sitting area in her bedroom suite.

"Damn. Nothing's really grabbing me. Let's try my mom's closet." Angie leads the way.

They try a couple of red tops as none of the dresses fit.

"Shit. The woman never fucking eats. I swear she's smaller than she was in high school. Let's try her backups in the spare wing."

21

"Geez. This is some crazy shit. She's a fucking *zero* now?" Harper having always been athletic has never ever fit even a two. "There must be a four somewhere in this house."

By the time they get situated, the main floor is full of swimmers giggling about teams, drivers, and captains. There will be four cars of four each and the walkers will be headed to local frat houses for their lists; which for the ladies entails gear from a rival sports team, or socks and underwear off some frat boys, maybe even digits or follows on Tinder. They would be Instagramming or Snapchatting the kissing and grabbing challenges.

Each team has one traveler ride plus two walker pods. Not more than twelve on each team. Four teams, one after party. Cheaters will pay. Last year's party netted "A Few Good Men" from the football team at the afterparty.

Expectations high, alcohol flowing, cell phones snapping; this year would be best ever. Hell every year was the new best ever. Official rules: *there are no rules*. Down the field we'll force our way—give a cheer for Stanford Red.

PART II

FRIDAY

Headline: UCPD investigating alleged sexual assault on campus affiliated Barge.

UCPD reported that it is currently investigating an assault in or near Cal's campus-affiliated Barge, which allegedly took place Friday morning, according to an alert issued Friday afternoon. The alert stated UCPD had received a report Friday about 2:45 a.m. that a female victim had allegedly been sexually assaulted, and transported to local medical facility for multiple injuries. The alert alleged the incident occurred at an affiliated location on campus sometime after midnight. The victim is not familiar with the suspects, according to the alert. Anyone with information about the incident, is asked to contact the UCPD Criminal Investigation Bureau at (510) 640-9843.

@Annon: Bitch wanted more, now cries RAPE — bull#$%&. #longlivethebarge

@MRS: Another alleged sexual assault on campus. When will it end?

@THR: End Rape on Campus needs you #joinE-ROC@UCB

Early AM

It's bright sunshine directly in her eyes that causes a stir in Frankie. She squints to see that she is not in her bed, sincerely confused as to whose bed she actually is in. Head banging, eyes burning. She realizes no cotton jammies or soft pillow anywhere in sight. It feels as though she is on a mattress, without a sheet?

An odd smell of burning something and molding something brings her to a sitting up position. "Holy Fuck Oley. Where am I?" She grimaces, then grabs for her flaming rear end. *Is there a knife in my ass?* The sensation of burning conflicts with pain from the wounding of a sharp blade. Is it a sting with throbbing or a fire with scorching hot flames licking at her bum? *What the hell is going on with me? This is not okay.* Tears begin to roll down her cheeks. Whether it's physical or emotional pain, she's not sure. Her eyes roll back into her head and she's out cold again.

Bright sunshine pours in through the window onto the wall in Beau's room; like golden ribbon. He stretches to an upright position and swells with pride. *I am gonna hit that water with gusto like no other today.* It's beep test day, and position coaches are fired up to get an A-squad announced. *My ass is ready.* He stretches his muscular arms toward the ceiling and rights himself. A glance at the time of day on the iPhone and he's gotten a sound and solid ten hours of shut eye—fuck yeah.

As he ties the fresh white Nike laces, he gets a slight notion that maybe he forgot to say "*thanks*" to Frankie last night. Meh. *I'll text her later to see what's the what.*

About an hour later, Frankie is reawakened by the searing pain in her bum area. *What the hell went down last night? And where the fuck am I right now?* She tries to stand, her knees go weak and she's bare-butt on a filthy mattress. As creepy as that quilt feels on her ass, she truly cannot get her footing to move off it. *What the actual fuck?*

Her cell phone is upside down on the floor near the side of the bed and she reaches for it, as she realizes her sides ache too. *Shit. What the fuck? I feel like I got hit by the proverbial truck last night.* It takes all of her willpower to grab the phone up and depress the home key. Nothing. Of course.
Dead battery. What time is it?

"Hey there sunshine—" a male voice, Frankie is alarmed.

WTF. Dewey? She turns to her left and sees his monstrous belly staring up at her. He is casually wrapped in a sheet around the shoulders portion of his body, but the belly and all the rest of the flab is jarring right in her eyeballs, making an indelible impression. She cannot un-see this. It is grim shit to say the least.

Before she can even form another thought, the door opens and John's head pops around the top.

"Dude, let's go. It's beep day." Real matter of fact.

Voices. Who is that talking? Where am I? Frankie is completely disoriented, in pain, and immobile.

27

"Oh. Hey Frankie. Pretty sure your dress is out here in the hall. Be right back. It's red, right?" John is jovial.

Fuck. Fuck, Shit, Damn. What the hell happened last night? Jane. Jane will know. I need my phone, but the pain. Why can I feel but not move?

"Black. My dress is black." Suddenly, Frankie must lay her head down to stop the room from spinning.

A large group of Cal boaters are gathering in the locker room to head out for practice. It is a big day, tryouts basically for who leads what boat, who might get cut from the squad.

"Dude. Thanks for the share." John slaps Beau on the shoulder just outside the locker room.

"Hey man," replies Beau. *Did he say share? Whatever.* "Let's nail this beep today. I'm gonna be all that and a box of chocolates when I make starting gold boat—stroke seat —watch me."

"Right on. Let's get it."

With that, the two head to their lockers to gear up. It's test, training and naming day. Both hoping for starting positions this fall. Beau used to be a part of the engine room, but naming on the event program is going to really impress his dad. Only the stroke seat gets that.

"Baker. What up?"

"Dudes. What a night. Beau, you the man. I heard that bitch put out 'til after three. Not shitting you, I came like four times. I swear." Baker is stretching the truth but these guys don't give a shit. "Fuck, man. She looked damn fine even before she went up to three."

"Hell yea, she's hot. That tight white ass. I didn't think I could hold her up for long but I got what I wanted." John pauses in honor of the memory. "Dewey's timing was key because I was so shit-faced, I almost dropped her in the hall." John wipes his forehead. "Some good shit you got there, Beau. Good shit."

"What the fuck?" Beau looks puzzled. His thoughts take him back to the second floor bathroom and the ultimate blow job Frankie had given him the night before. *But didn't they call it a night about 11?* He was sure he had kissed her goodnight on the forehead—still a bit creeped out about kissing a girl whose mouth is full of his jizz— and then walked her back to her friends on the dance floor.

"Get it ladies," he'd said, as he bid his farewell to Frankie and her gal pals, headed back to his place for some beauty sleep. "I got an early day tomorrow. You ladies get your groove on and I'll see you around."

Before midnight that night, he was snuggled up to his stuffed lion Brandy gave him before he left Dexter that summer. He tried to keep that thing under his pillow so the guys wouldn't razz him. Having someone to hold in the night started to feel really good after that summer of sleepovers.

"Leo the Lion will be with you at Cal—til we're back together at Xmas—I love you, B&B4Ever." Somehow, Brandy had managed to get all that on the one inch tag attached to Leo's ass.

God he missed her. She had the softest tits he'd ever known. Well, the *only* tits he'd ever known before Cal. But her thick, floral-scented red hair dancing across his face when she straddled him on his twin race car bed back home—craving her—boner busting up through denim while she rocked side to side and back to front. He could not wait until the day came when he'd take her virginity.

The summer before college, they were allowed "sleep overs" after Brandy had explained to Beau's mother about how she was a good Catholic girl, waiting until she and Beau were married or some shit. Unbelievable, his Mom never told Dad Brandy slept over. Even harder to figure he never popped his head into the bedroom before leaving for work in the mornings to see the duo pretzel twisted together between the sheets.

Weekends they'd set an alarm and Brandy would sneak out no later than 7am—except that one time they'd hit snooze too many times and overslept until nearly 11. Mom had been so slick with the story about how Dad needed to accompany her to the farmer's market to see some $200 hand-carved stool she wanted. Especially crazy Dad bought that story because Mom was the ever frugal, couponing, "*I'll have liver and onions if it's two-for-one'*" kind of shopper extraordinaire. *A $200 stool?* He smiled wide thinking back, then snapped out of it.

"No seriously guys. What's up?" His mind is back in the locker room.

"Dude, let's go. Coach says ten minutes early is *late*." Off they are to join the sixty-five other fall boater hopefuls.

Baker brings up the rear. He has little or no chance of making it on a boat roster. Hanging with these bad ass bros is what's in it for him. And that fine tail the boat house always has ambling the dance floor at the barge.

Three vans are lined up out back of the Simpson Center for transport from campus to the bay for practice. John and Beau are in the first van. No sign of Dewey as they roll away. Beau looks across to ask John about last night, but he's already asleep.

"Beau man, you the shit. That curling crew—some fine ass," Raul chimes in as he climbs into a seat behind Beau. Raul is Beau's archrival vying for the top spot stroke seat. His fist is literally in Beau's face for a bump.

"Fuck you, Raul. You're going down today. Don't even get at me," he replies. *What the fuck is all the hype about anyways?* On that note, he's sawing logs until the moment the driver hollers for everyone to get out.

Friday classes are seriously full of freshmen only. No class means sleep in through breakfast and save another 500 calories. It's nearly 2 pm and Jane is starving, unclear as to why she has not heard from Frankie yet. She cannot still be sleeping. I wonder if she went to brunch with that bitch Marla. Transfers cause such a shit load of drama on and off the ice.

"I swear," she says to her mirror, "I will flip my shit if they went without me. Fuck it, I am texting Beth. They probably already ate but I'll make them go to International House with me anyways." Practice at 4 on Fridays is such a fucking pain in the ass. "Never, ever do we get a long weekend."

Beth and Anne meet up with a few other curling crew freshmen Friday morning and swiped into the dining hall at Kerr. They can sit and eat to their heart's content on the freshman Cal1 card swipe, while the freshies jet off to class. Anne agreed to let a couple of freshmen take her scooter anyways so she and Beth will have to wait about an hour until they get out of class and back with it.

"Beth, what gives? That ass wipe, Dewey, is a fat, fucking lard ass and he is out every weekend with a different girl." She is particularly annoyed this morning because she counts each and every calorie while that fat ass burps his way to celebrity. "I swear, boaters on this campus are highly over rated."

"I agree," says Beth. "But free alcohol is free alcohol, so it was a good night overall."

"Agreed." Anne is back to grab just a small squeeze of frozen yogurt from the dispenser.

"What time did they say they'd be back with the scooter? I need you to scoot me to Versailles this morning. Last night that fucking punch bin literally ate my gel polish off. What the fuck do you think was *in that shit*?" Beth is biting at what's left of the passion pink ring finger nail.

"No telling. But free is free like you said." They laugh and check back to their respective cell phone screens reviewing the snaps from the evening.

"Holy shit. Is Kanye really cheating on Kim?"

"Beau. Great party last night." Gerome is a transfer.

"Seriously man. You dipped way too early. We were just getting going at midnight." The guys are readying boats for put in to the bay.

"Hell yeah, that midnight hour baby," exclaimed Tom. "Bitches be throwing themselves at us all night long, but midnight, ooh-ee that's when shit gets started."

"You missed the red parade man. Stanford bitches be off the chains," Gerome adds.

"The Barge was the bomb—but it's time to get a few more private spaces on the first floor man. Dragging them up the stairs is a bitch, if you know what I'm saying." Derek, ever the ladies man. "Think about it. Bitches be complaining about them stairs all night. A few more futons in the kitchen area is all I'm talking about. Get us some soft surfaces in the groove areas too, you know, alongside of the dance floor, it's dark enough."

"And I ain't gonna get whatchew be giving out back on them moldy ass fuckin thirty-year-old mattresses," added Gerome.

"Shut up or put up Derek. You want to buy a few futons? We'll take 'em." John strides in to add his two cents. "But I have to agree, getting up those freaking stairs nearly had me like, 'I cannot hold this bitch up any more,' before I even got my shit done."

"After a round or two for them bitches, it's like, just leave one up there and hit that," called Tom. "Like why bother with all the up and down shit. Just get the one bitch up there and take your fucking turn man. It ain't no big thang. Not like any of you chumps can tell a tight ass from a wet pussy from your fucking babysitter's apple pie."

"What the fuck man. Don't be talking apple pie. I'm fucking starving right now."

The boaters spent their early weekday morning hours on the water, and are rewarded with a fine spread Fridays at Skates on the Bay afterwards. It's testing day and the crew be hype.

Beth is getting her gel-manicure fixed and Anne has the white tips being applied toe by toe as the phones begin to buzz. "Of course, it's Jane. She must need something."

"You get mine. I don't want to ruin my nails," Beth instructs Anne. As suspected, it's Jane. "Wassup," is all it says. Just like the screen on Anne's phone.

"I swear, she simply hits copy and paste on her cell when she needs something. She probably sends it to the entire squad just waiting on peeps to offer her a ride. It's not our fault she fucking dumped her scooter into the bay. Why the fuck did she ride it all the way down there anyways? For some weed? Honestly. It's not my turn to save her."

Beth hit delete on both phones and switched back to the latest People magazine on her lap.

"How does Katie Holmes even get hot for Jamie Foxx when she can have *any man* on the planet? Seriously Brad Pitt is available, and if she must have a black bone, The Weekend just split with his model-ass bitch."

"Hey. Did you see Frankie last night? She was lit," Beth says. "I didn't ask Jane on the ride back but so much for the buddy system with them, right? Lit and loaded as fuck."

"You *ever* leave me at that dump and I will kill you, Beth," scolds Anne. "Not kidding. That place is *disgusting*, even in the dark— but that free alcohol calls." They both fall back into laughter and snap story reviews.

Frankie

Frankie read something not long ago about the egotistical mind. "You're worthless. You never get anything right. You seriously fucked that up last night." But no true or graphic memories of the night came to her. *Should I text Beau or wait for him to text? Did anything happen? Did I really wake up naked in bed with Dewey this morning?* That horrific thought made her pull the pillow over her head and roll over back to sleep.

Jane

Bitches, answer my text. "I swear I'll call that transfer bitch and ditch you all," she mumbled out loud, as she checked the fridge one last time for anything edible. The smell outta the damn thing made her angry at herself for even looking. Fucking dried carrots. *Did I read somewhere on Facebook that carrots are actually sugary and fattening? Fuck it, I'm starving.* Ranch dressing from two apartments two years ago and a handful of carrots. *How many calories is ranch, and what is a serving?*

Marla

Marla knew there was still a chance that someone would find out that she called in about the party to 9 1 1. Someone at some point could still have caller ID and cops would swarm her apartment like on TV. It was quite likely she'd be forced to start talking. She lay on her bed wondering why it had been more than 24 hours and no one had followed up from that call last night.

"Emergency Operations Berkeley. Is this an emergency?"

"Well, I. Yes, I think I saw an emergency. I mean, there's this girl."

"Are you hurt? Can you tell me your name and where you are calling from?"

"No, it's not me. And not here. Well I was there. Wait, can you just send an ambulance to the Barge?"

"Ok ma'am, if you are calling about a female victim on the corner of, well that barge place, then I think we already have it covered."

"Are you sure?" Marla was terrified that with caller ID and what not this woman might be mistaken.

"We have an ambulance already out on a call to this Barge you speak of ma'am. Second call on this unless you believe there is something happening at this moment with someone other than a twenty something white female."

Marla hung up quickly. *Takes sixty seconds to trace a call right?*

Edgar

Edgar cannot get back to his room quick enough. He has too much at stake to let this little snag in the rug catch his footing. *Gotta fuckin shut down this Andre motha-fucker.*

He checks his phone for the umpteenth time and still no GroupMe. *Fuck it. I'm starting it.*

"BFW." Code for Be-Fucking-Ware. He'll get to a laptop quickly and post.

It's another block to his apartment and he starts a mental checklist: *Email re: Andre. Dude about to go rogue and talk to police. Deny telling anything (or throw Beau under the bus. Frankie was his problem being he'd fuckin invited her???). Launder every single piece of bedding, clothing, area rug... EVERYTHING near the scene with her last night. EAT something, I am fucking starving.*

Fuckin Beau, inviting female freaking student athletes takes finesse; you cannot invite the bitch YOU KNOW HAS ALREADY DONE THE ENTIRE FOOTBALL FUCKIN
SQUAD. Total recipe for disaster cause those fuckin mental whores eventually fucking snap. Bitch prolly called the cops once she hit third floor last night and shit.

In addition to the GroupMe messages, when shit really hits the fan the gang must communicate in code. DDD deny deny deny; CK – coach knows; LOL – leave on lights (loosely translated you need to be on the alert...can be relating to boats, babes, or barge activities...just lay low).

Any one were to ask BFW – big fuckin whoop; DDD – dude duck down; CK – check; LOL – laugh out loud.

BFW was used sparingly, and included the need to take cover, say nothing, and check for an electronic update via your email created specifically for top secret information.

Only guys in the inner circle are privy to this code. Fake Gmail accounts are setup in or around your sophomore year with the team, once an upperclassman deems you worthy. This Gmail account is used only in extreme cases where you believe your phone, student email, or workout logs and RPE are being summoned by coaching staff. The police questioning most definitely warranted a BFW.

Edgar took the back stairs up two at a time. He had some shit to get done. As he looks out from the stairwell window his eye catches a couple of cops out back by the dumpster. *Fuck. Get the fucking sheets and get the fuck outta here.*

He's in and out in less than three minutes.

It's just a couple blocks to Cal Suds on College. He thankfully remembered his half roll of quarters, alas has forgotten the detergent. *Fuck, that's $5 for the soap, fuckin gonna have to hit Derby for more quarters.* The extra-large load is finally spinning nicely when he dials home.

"Hey Ma, it's me." Mother is pleased to hear her son's voice; instant *valium effect* on son hearing mom swoon in delight.

"Oh. What a lovely surprise darling, your father isn't home…" she's filling his tainted mind with the comfy sound of home. Talking to her always calmed him as she filled the line with "…Aunt Edith's recent surgery, dad taking all day at the grocery

39

store, dinner would be late again, all his father's fault, thank heavens we are not having guests." Home will always be home. Sigh.

"Honey, I thought the team does your laundry," his mother chimed thru the cell phone, when he had said he was just calling to chat about two hours ago when this process began.

It is a few minutes before he realizes that the dyer is not heating up. *Mother fuckin whore—that asshole owner still hasn't fixed the dryers—he's been here for-fuckin-ever trying to dry these damn sheets and towels.*

Well screw the pooch. He'd completely forgotten to email the group after the BFW. *FML.*

"Gotta go Mom, tell Dad hi." He didn't wait to hear her add "kiss kiss or love you."

Executive decision time. He switches the load to another dryer and pops in next door to use Wi-Fi. He's greeted at Sacks by a couple of ladies in red dresses.

"Hey, aren't you from that house?" Stanford female asks. "My friend lost her dress there and we need to get back in but there's a bunch of cops there."

"Nope. Wrong guy. Not me. I don't know who you are and I don't have a dress."

"Oh, yes you do. I saw you dragging an unconscious chick up the stairs last night."

"Fuck you bitch. I never saw you, you never saw me." Edgar broke into a cold sweat. No Wi-Fi here. He needed to get underground and fast. He bolted out and in a slight jog made it to Beau's apartment on Hillegass. No answer. *FUCK.*

"Can I help you son?" Some white-haired neighbor literally appeared out of nowhere.

"No. No thanks. I was just looking for a friend." He was doing his best to remain calm.

"Your friend is probably out with his pals. It is Friday night after all." *So matter-of-fact those elderly.*

"Thanks." *YES. Free slices at Fatty's Pizza on Fridays 4 to 7.* Quick-footed he headed towards Telegraph Ave.

The usual suspects are gathered at Fatty's. Boaters at two big top tables, football taking up an entire back room. Beers are flowing and the pizza is free with a Student Athlete Cal One card. Perks of the elite.

Edgar comes in hot, takes stock of who is who and sitting where. Who can he trust with this? He has got to shut down the threat, and now. Andre's officially had a three hour jump on him; fuckin laundry. *Well, fuck me, I left that shit in the dryer?*

No sign of Beau, who is currently sitting Barge house manager under the bylaws. *Fuck him. He fuckin dipped out and left that bitch unattended.* He'll have to wing it with Baker and Raul for now. *Not going down alone on this shit...*

"Hey man," full-mouthed Raul.

"Hey." Baker.

"Time to grab a bunker gentlemen—we got a problem." Edgar's ability to keep it calm was failing him. The encounter at Sacks threw him off like never before. "Cops at the house," he said, under his breath.

"Dude, relax. Grab a slice. Whaddup?" Raul spits just a bit of cheese onto Edgar's chest, unintentionally.

"Fuckin serious, Raul. We gotta get underground—follow me." As he begins to walk away he realizes neither Baker nor Raul have moved a muscle. "Fuckin *now*."

"Who fuckin died and made you the boss of shit?" Baker.

"No shit. Relax and fuckin eat you asshole." Raul.

Coach Reid was looking at his roster taking a mental roll call when he realized there was no Frankie in the room.

"Where the hell is Frankie?" Coach Reid was sick to death of these damn spoiled little rich bitch curlers. Once, just once, could they give him a truly dedicated athlete to show Canada they were not the only country to produce a curling super star? While the sport did not require a shit ton of strategy, a consistent athlete with decent physical skill and a high degree of mental toughness was all he needed.

Disrespectful, tardy, back-talking prima-donnas was the lot again this year. *It's back to Scotland next season if this shit continues.*

I've had it. "Seriously ladies. Next athlete to skip a Friday practice is off the squad. She damned well better have a doctor's note. You three tell her that too." He was staring at Beth, Anne, and Jane. All of whom were dumbfounded as to where in the world was Frankie.

"All of you, hit the weight room. Marla, you're skip today with that bunch." Pointing to the trio. Being new, coach had no idea if this gal could hack it, but he was going to send a message about missing practice.

"Holy shit, this is sooo not cool. Frankie is gonna fucking freak the fuck out if Marla taps her for skip at regionals," Anne chimed in.

"No shit Sherlock," added Beth.

Jane

Jane was beginning to get a sick stomach feeling. It wasn't just the rancid dressing she ate with petrified carrots an hour ago, but from the thought of where and when she last saw Frankie. Taking a drink from the mouth of a Boater near the kitchen as she dipped out the back door— where was her dream boat Beau, and why oh why drink from another guy's mouth? She was glad no one noticed as she slithered out the back way.

Sure. She had frolicked off out the back way of the barge last night without her *buddy*, but she was sick of playing third wheel to Frankie and her boys. From day one freshmen year, it seemed she was destined to be a wing man; she was ready for flying on her own this year. Fuck those boaters. She'd danced one or two songs with A and B then headed to Kaps, the on campus watering hole frequented by students and Berkeley locals, where she was certain her new crush would be grinding.

Frankly, the barge was no place for size 8 jeans; the twos and fours were just too easily tanked and tempting—ditsy drunks being such easy prey for dumb jocks. She was by no means fat, but the collegiate male brain it seemed only had eyes for small, drunk, easy marks. That age old scenario was not going to change anytime soon, and she was ready for a bit of appreciation outside of the campus jug heads. She'd wandered on to the dance floor over at Kaps and let her pal James know she was ready to take it to the next level.

Jane and James

James was a sturdy black man with great hands. Twice Jane had creamed herself into needing a change of undies just dancing with him in the darkness on the sticky floor at Kaps. His magic fingers had a way of working through the wall of cotton or denim and panties without fail. Tonight she was ready in a super short LBD, bring on the fire.

It was high time she learned a little bit more about James, as well as develop a better understanding of the phrase 'go black and never go back.' Was it truth or urban legend? Should she brave it and ask to see his place or take him back to hers?

Having her own room this year was a luxury she had yet to take full advantage of. Shit. The short dress and his handsy ways, they may not make it past the staircase to the street; she was hot just thinking about him. *Am I attracted to him, or is it just the orgasms? Would that just fucking blow my mom's mind to bring a black man home for turkey dinner this year?*

She was laughing like a crazy cat lady to herself as she took the short voyage off Durant and up to Kaps.

She was up the stairs and working her way towards the back when someone grabbed her from behind. *Holy shit...what the...*

"Hey baby, it's just you and me tonight." *God he sounds just like John Legend.*

James held her in a reverse bear hug and began sucking on her ear lobe. Oh My God. This is it. She swirled around grabbing his crotch at the same time she thrust her tongue in his mouth. After a few bumps from passersby, they decided to take their business back to his place.

He had a place. Check. He had a job. Check 2. Jane remembered quite a bit about the apartment and its colorful textile strewn across the walls; but not much from the beginning of her night with Frankie. Turned out James was an assistant manager at the Verizon store on Shattuck; a new iPhone was defs in her weekend plans.

Not once did she think another thought about Frankie until now. Where the hell was she? And how dare she ditch practice less than a month before regionals?

The foursome had a pact—if one ditched—they all pitched, and stick to one story agreed to by all. Here she was spotting Marla at the weight room and for what? *More of Frankie's bullshit? Probably a swell bitch session about how she was not committed enough to tell Coach R to stuff it, ditch and go find Frankie. Fuck her. She fucking never even called me today.*

Marla

Marla was not at all excited about her new found position. She'd curled only one match at Davis before transferring and really truly did not enjoy it. Her father was a Canadian national player and her mom was such a freaking jock that sports was not optional in parochial school, but expected. Curling was way less hours and not a contact sport—hell most of the time she only had to participate two or three months out of the year being that ice was so scarce in NorCal.

That one summer the family spent in Saskatchewan. It seemed like it was going to make everyone happy that I even put those ridiculous shoes on. I was twelve and Dad made such a big deal about it. He had always not-sosecretly wanted a son and my sister and I both knew it. She was the ultimate girl jock—track in fall, basketball in the winter, and lacrosse any time there was a chance to play in a tournament. Our high school didn't have lacrosse but by golly Amy found teams to travel with. Honestly, why hadn't she simply signed up for lacrosse because at the end of the day maybe one or two people on the entire team ever touched the ball? Amy would run up and down the entire field to score without ever looking to pass or anything.

Fudge. Today was going to be the day her weak ass idea caught up to her. I hate curling. I hate the shoes. I hate the ice. I hate the freaking forty-pound freaking flat ass bowling ball of a rock.

Again, that Saskatchewan summer. I sort of thought it would be funny to go and push dad's prized possession into a gutter but nope, straight up the ice it went. No brooming, no planning, just landed square in the center of the target. Bad idea genes.

From that day forward, Dad spoke to Marla only as his prodigy. "My best gal," he'd say. "Let's get our *rocks* on Mar." He'd laugh out loud at his funny self.

Off they would go to the rink. Most of the time he spent demonstrating so Marla had it pretty keen, an entire Saturday or Sunday of no chores. An hour drive to the rink grabbing Starbucks on the way being Tim Horton's had yet to make it to the States, followed by In and Out burgers on the way home. Sometimes it was a full eight hour day away from Mom and the nagging weekend chore list.

"Leave her Marge, she carried the stones today and we're both wiped. Did good today kid." her dad would explain. "You'll get it next time. Drop the hammer, ya know." There was always next time.

Why oh why did she still have to be involved in sports? At eighteen, were you not deemed an adult, and for cripes sake she was nineteen and at a new campus. "You'll have a set of nice friends first day," assured Marge. "Good sportsmanship is something you'll take with you your whole life missy—team player—not always thinking about yourself." Since when, if ever, did Marla think about herself? Her whole life revolved around if, what, and where her parents might be able to brag about this or that. Just once she'd hoped there would come a day when someone, *anyone* were to ask, "so Marla, what is it you would like to do/see/eat/make of your life?" Not today.

Completely lost in her thoughts, Jane was on her second, maybe fourth rep when the weight bar clanged to the floor.

"What the fuck, bitch?" Marla quickly knelt down to rerack the load. *That was a close one.*

"Sorry. Sorry. Uhm where were you?" she inquired timidly.

"Fuckin *where were **you**,* bitch?" was Jane's reply.

Frankie

Frankie tried twice to get up from the bed and find her phone, but whatever the heck she drank last night was really sticking with her. Damned Jungle Juice. I should have known those cheap boat bastards would use Vodka of the Gods or some shit. Why did I accept the red cup after—after—what the hell happened last night?

Beau and the boys at practice

Beau was uptight as hell about the change in attitude from Coach Carter. He'd all but assured Beau he had the position as long as he worked hard and proved he wanted it. Early bed all of pre-season, extra hours in the weight room. Hell, if he could have additional strokes on the water he would have. Which is why his mother used her savings to buy him the *Stamina* conditioning rowing machine for his room—he'd put in plenty of sweat equity there. *What the fuck does this guy want from me?*

As the boaters loaded their paddles and stacked things up, dark clouds rolled in over their heads from the city. Beau and a few others too cool for stacking were still inside at the buffet.

"Okay men. Let's finish up in here and meet back at the docks," Coach Carr bellowed. Carr was just the assistant. *We got a couple minutes* Beau thought to himself.

"Damn bro, you just got that plate. Better choke it back in a quick sec or your ass is getting the grab." Jones had just stuffed two large tablespoons of mashed potatoes in his mouth before spraying Beau with that message and tater bits.

Well known to boaters long before season one at Cal Boating is the fact that Coach Carr had a boorish taste for the ass grasp. Last one out the locker room, to the bus, off the field. The saying was "last one, best one" or the ever popular, "clutch of too much" nomenclature.

Golly, thought Beau, *finish up the smoked salmon and divine cheesecake slice, or leave it and avoid the noid?* The only other thing on his mind was that position announcement. Beau was truly torn over this thought.

Coach Carter appeared out of nowhere and spun a chair a quick 180 just across from where Beau was eating. He straddled the chair and crossed his arms across the upholstered back.

"Beauregard Pierce. Fucking bad-ass mother-fucker you think you are, dontcha?" spat Coach. "I am going to ask you this question *one time,* and I want a straight answer. Were you, or were you not, at a party at the barge last night?"

Beau, amid an extra-large bite, unable to swallow seeing Coach swoop in on him like this, reached for a napkin from the seat next to him to dump the load. *Beauregard. Fuck him. He knows it's Beau.* Clearing his throat, he managed, "Sir."

"Don't fucking, sir, me you little prick. Answer the question. *Yes or no*, were you at the fucking barge partying last night?" he barked.

"Well, uh, yes, but just for an hour or so. I was not drinking, sir." Beau could hear his twelve-year-old voice squeaking out across the table as softly as possible. He could also feel the immediate presence of perspiration on his forehead—lying brought on an instantaneous flow of fluid down the sides of his face. *Un-Fucking Believable.* As he wiped his brow, he remembered the salmon in the napkin as hollandaise smeared across and down. *Fuck*, he was now a smeared mess.

"Fucking figures. You bastards *know* you have a testing day, *know* about the 24/48 rule. *Know* my fucking ass is on the line with this shit—you figure you're above the law, dontcha? Mother fuckers." And with that, Coach was up and out.

Right behind him was Coach Carr. "Let's go man. Hit the vans," he clamored at Beau.

Not another word was spoken that day about who'd be steering what boat. Seagulls screeching across the parking lot being the only sound the boaters heard as they sat loaded in three vans heading back to campus. Coaches huddled on the deck of the restaurant in conversation. After what felt like an hour, Coach Carr climbed on the bus with a slight "fuckin-ay" under his breath.

Holly

Another truly torn individual that Friday morning was Holly. Holly's lush blond hair and simply sweet demeanor was all folks ever remembered about her from the barge. Unlike so many babes at the barge, Holly was NOT a student athlete. She'd irresponsibly attended a party last night at the barge—it was a school night for heaven's sake —at about midnight when the red dresses arrived, an entirely different vibe filled the room. *Red dresses really did brighten up the place.*

These must be some Stanford ladies because every incoming freshman at Cal learned the rules—absolutely no red clothing, not even socks or underwear—an annual bonfire near the bay early fall took care of any trace reds. Holly left the barge before a ruckus began over it; these ladies had a look of determination on their heels. No escort tonight. She decided she just wanted out of here.

Home safe in less than nine minutes she texted her sister the ceremonious √—their previously agreed upon code— it was 12:17 am. She knew her baby sis would be sound asleep in Florida being three hours ahead, but she felt better just knowing that someone somewhere always got the message when she was home safe in her room. Holly's younger sister used the check mark check-in way more than she—she was only in grade eleven but out to parties nearly every weekend. They had made the pact summer before Holly's freshman year at Cal, 'you never know' they'd agreed.

Holly had befriended a few athletes her freshman year in a Lit class, and was highly regarded as untouchable to the boaters. A beautiful blonde Floridian in the front row, plenty of guys jockeyed for a seat next to her and tried their best one-liners. Ever the friendly southern belle, Holly was pleasant and open about the fact that she was a non-drinker, a self-described 'virgin, waiting til marriage for sexual encounters—not on any sort of birth control.' Her pastor had counseled her on the importance of being upfront and open about this as she headed off to the great wild west university. 'Always best to let new friends know who you are and what you believe in right up front,' he'd explained. 'Saves so much time and any potential misunderstandings that may arise in social settings.' Pastor Phil was a fountain of knowledge. A man Holly trusted with her life.

Even the girls Holly met got much the same, 'how do you do' in an initial meet and greet.

Word spread quickly on that note. Any 'no pill chick' was well known to an incoming class, and Holly was also lead role in a sort of 'hands off pact' by boaters and ballers of all sports. She'd saved half dozen or more of them from suspension for low GPA by tutoring and sharing her writing assignments. 'Sister Holly' was how many guys on campus referred to her.

As a freshman, Holly was giddy at the chance to party at a frat house. Tutoring a few hunky idiots an hour or two a week opened doors to her that were unheard of back in the tiny town of Monteverde Florida. St. Mary's Academy was worlds away from this mecca of muscle-bound maleness. Being a junior, the allure had worn off, but she still frequented the Barge on occasion just so she could report to her inquiring sister she'd been out.

Oh what learning there was to garner at this house of male Gods at California's premier public institution for higher education. She'd certainly seen, heard, and closely encountered enough skin and grind to understand her place in this dwelling. Stories she'd shared with sis back home kept her lying awake many nights grappling with whether or not this whole virgin thing was causing her to miss out on too much.

Lots of girls had pressed her about her surreptitious position in the house. How did she have the entire Barge always treating her like a lady and with such respect? It was well-known and often mocked the way the guys always made sure Holly had a clean cup, plenty of attention, and a sober member walk her home before midnight. What was her secret?

Three van loads of boaters unloaded at the back of the Simpson center and no one was speaking. Without a word, half headed to the weight room, the other half to scooters parked out front. Beau and few followers headed towards Sproul.

Coach Carter stormed up the stairs to grab his jacket. "I am fucking outta here. Carr, you're in charge."

"Sir, uhm—" Carr began.

"No fuckin way I am goin' down on this sinking fucking ship. I'm headed to Willards' office to hand in my letter. Fuckin west coast assholes. I have plenty of options out East."

Coach Carter was cruising on about two hours sleep. He'd had one too many call outs at 2 and 3 am about the boaters and their schoolboy antics. Last night was a call from the fucking medical center. Fucking idiots had some sort of run-in with 'red dresses' and he was freakin' done.

"That's it," he'd hollered at his wife, Janine, sometime around 4am. "We are headed back East. Just like you've always wanted. Happy? Fuckin mother-fuckers fuckin tryna ruin my fuckin reputation—asshole little shits."

"Honey. You'll wake the children," was all Janine could muster. She'd been his punching bag for the past four seasons while raising their two toddlers basically on her own. She rolled back to sleep with the comfortable thought of having family around to help soon enough. Boston was her home.

Holly was headed back to her apartment that Friday morning after a volunteer hour at St. Mark's; serving the homeless and People's Park residents a warm breakfast. It was nearly eleven and she wanted to catch The View this morning because Michelle Obama was a guest host. Looking down at her cell for the exact time, out of the corner of her eye she saw a bright red something nearly hit by a blue Toyota at College and Durant. *Holy crap*. Seeing that red dress briefly took her thoughts back to the Barge.

"Hey. Can I help you up?" Holly had run into the street without looking both ways but couldn't help but grab for this noodle of a human being who seemed to have no sense of awareness whatsoever. "Look, you gotta get up.
You're in the middle of the street," she pleaded.

"Hey, can you hear me?" Holly's heart rate quickened. Was this girl *dead* from '*almost* getting hit?' Thankfully the Toyota pulled over to help. She called out to the driver. "You didn't hit her, did you?" Honestly at that moment Holly was not sure what she had or had not seen.

"No way. She almost walked into me though. It's *her fault*.
I swear I had to swerve *out* of *her* way," said the young Asian man.

"What the fuck?"

"Listen. I didn't mean it like that. Help me out here—can you help me get her out of the street?" Holly was pleading and apologizing and trying her damndest to get this girl up and outta the road. It took both of them to prop her up on the curb before they realized yes she was breathing but no, not coherent.

Holly was torn. What is the right thing to do in this situation? "Should we call 911?"

"Where did she come from?" asked the guy. "And where is she going in this little number?" his eyes were attempting to not see the bulging of the breasts out the front of the red number stretched awkwardly across Frankie's limp body.

"How should I know?" Holly was completely out of breath. "Can you take her to the hospital?" she inquired.

"Shit no. I didn't do nothing. She ain't my problem and I ain't in no mood for this right now."

"Ah right. Well, she isn't mine either, and I am not in the mood myself since you're asking." Politely Holly tried to regain regular breathing. "Listen. Help me get her up, or at least to that bench there."

With both arms and both legs unresponsive, getting the lifeless co-ed to a bench required assistance from two additional passersby.

"You can't just leave her there." Random assistant number one judgingly reported.

"Who is she?" asked the other. Holly was beginning to feel like the Lord had just handed her an unbearable task here; a test of sorts. *Do the right thing* chimed the voice inside her head.

"Look. I just saw her go down in the middle of the street. I don't know her any better than you all do—and frankly you almost hit her—*and* you have a car. I think if anyone here is responsible for this gal, it's you." Holly eyed the driver. "I have to go, I'm late."

"Late for what?" chirped Frankie.

"Holy shit. She's alive," assistant number two whispered.

Inside of seven seconds, Frankie recited her name and her address before dropping right back into the oblivion she'd been in.

"What the hell was that?" asked the Toyota driver.

"Crimeny. I don't know," Holly replied. "Sorta came out like a first grader is told to recite his or her name and address at Safety School."

"Huh?" Holly could tell that the Asian guy was not a graduate of any grade school safety program, but no time for explanation. She had to convince him to help get this girl to her home.

"She said 2756 Benvenue. That's less than three blocks. Just help me get her into your car and we'll drop her there," pleaded Holly. *Why oh why do I get myself into messes like this*?

It would take all four of them to get Frankie into the Toyota, and less than a mile later to pull up to the house.

Holly realizes, somehow, they have to get this girl inside.

Frankie

She woke about noon needing to pee. Not one single solid remembrance of Thursday night past the couch toss. Sheesh. *What now?*

A hot shower and a run? *I cannot get up from this bed. Every bone in my body aches, and that nagging anal itch—is it an itch or pain?* She's really gotta pee. *Up, up. Come on gurl. Get up and...just another step...phew.* Made it to the porcelain perch. That's when the true panic hit her.

What the fuck. Is that blood? My period was just last week. Her thoughts are causing her a screaming headache.

Toilet paper feels like sand paper—and that sand paper is bringing up some pretty nasty blackish red stains. Well no. There was black and now bright red wipes coming up. *Oh My God what is wrong with my butt hole?* Pulling herself to a standing position for a second time in five minutes takes so much energy that Frankie can barely get the seven feet from bathroom to her bedroom door. *What if...ohmyGod what is wrong with me...it hurts... bleeding?* Tears roll down her face as she thinks about every girl she has ever read about blacking out. *Is this it? Am I ruined? How can I ever ever face...what if I was raped? ... Who the hell was I even with last night? Oh please no. Make it stop. Let this all be a really bad dream and wake me up!* She grabs for the door as it swings and provides zero support, she catches herself from a serious fall. *Where did I put my phone? Gotta call Jane.* Three giant steps for mankind and she's to the bed where she falls on to her familiar Harry Styles purple pillow case and sleeps like the dead.

It was nearly 7PM Friday evening before Frankie could make another go for the toilet. *Fuck. Ouch. WTF is all over the bedding? What time is it? Crap what day is it? Did I miss practice? Why did no one wake me up for practice? Where the hell is Jane? What the fuck happened to my room? Somebody please make the room stop spinning. I am starving, where am I? What the fuck is that red slinky number doing on the floor of my bathroom? Who's been in my room? I hate red and that shit is banned on campus for fuck's sake...who in the hell has been in my room with RED?* Anger seemed to increase the pounding in her head.

I need to sleep this off. And with that she dropped to the floor in the bathroom. Grabbing for her bathrobe off the back of the door, to serve as pillow and blanket in one.

Back to Holly

Holly could not stop thinking about that red dress. It did not seem to fit that girl at all. Odd choice of attire for mid-morning on a Friday. Surely it was a walk of shame situation...the girl looked a lot like a snotty brunette who was flirting at the Barge last night...but wasn't she wearing black? Jeez, for a school that supposedly takes a pretty high GPA to get in, there sure were an awful lot of stupid people here, she decided.

Back to Shark Tank. Thank heavens Holly's sister had recorded The View and Ellen today because the entire day involved getting that dip in to her house, on to a bed, and out of her hands. Bugger that she'd have to wait til going home at Thanksgiving to see the Michelle Obama appearances. *Maybe I'll ask one of the guys to help me watch a replay on the computer.* The guys were always bragging about how they didn't pay for cable but watched whatever show they wanted on some streaming site.

It was nearly 9:45 and she simply could not focus on the deals the sharks were negotiating. Should she go back and check to make sure that girl was actually okay? Guilt plagued her. She stood up from her chips and salsa and grabbed for her keys. It's just about three blocks over, maybe five, I'll be back by 10:15. *Who needs another smart lightbulb anyways?* She flipped off the TV.

Berkeley PD had plenty of action Thursday through Saturday. Not to discount Taco Tuesday but that had at least some food in the theme, resulting in markedly less drunk and disorderly call outs. The cross-over between campus police and Berkeley City PD was a constant thorn. Kids drink, kids destroy, kids suck—when the kids appeared downtown, it always meant extra paperwork.

Did the crime occur on or off campus property? Did he say or she say, alcohol almost always involved. *I am getting too old for this job*, thought Detective Monroe. He watched as Chief Orzo pulled into his spot off MLK Jr Way. Another breezy fall Friday morning, students back on campus meant never a dull moment. *I'll give him a head start in.*

The Police Chief

Thursday's chaos bothered the Chief the most. *Back in my day, Thursday was considered a school night.* He strode past the break room to his office. First thing Friday morning and he'd already had calls in from two coaches, two patrol officers, and the fucking AD at Cal. Carter and the AD he'd heard of. "Nancy. Who is Coach Zender?" He asked before heading to his chair.

"Sir. I believe it's the head coach of Stanford women's swim and dive teams, sir." Nancy looked and sounded a bit nervous. Orzo looked up from the pink slips to take in her facial expression.

"What is it, Nancy?" he inquired.

"It doesn't sound good, sir. I think you should talk to Monroe and Smythe before returning her call."

"Thank you, Nancy." With that, he headed straight for his top drawer and grabbed the Tums. He dropped two into his cup of black coffee. Not that he intended to even drink this crap, station brew, but it made him feel like he was 'taking action against the rumble beginning to rise in his belly.'

Detective Monroe strode in a moment later to inquire with Nancy.

"What's the rattle I am hearing about a few Stanford students at a party here last night?" Detective Monroe worked a shit ton of overtime and always gave the most accurate overview. Unlike others who would spend fifteen minutes telling you about the hair and eye color of the victim or assailant, as if that mattered to the Chief.

Just the facts please was his motto.

Minutes later Monroe and Smythe were in the conference room. The white board was nearly covered with names and times and circles and arrows—BARGE was scrolled center and bold in the diagram. *Shit, not this place again.*

"Good Morning, Chief." Monroe.

"Morning, sir." Smythe.

"Cut the niceties fellas. What in the hell is the BARGE center of this time?" barked Orzo. "Just the facts."

"Not a shit ton of facts just yet, sir. Mostly, she said and he said. Patrol shut 'er down about 2 on site, but we got a couple a perps in the station about 1:27 am."

Monroe spoke up. "Plenty of interviews but no statements yet." A moment later Monroe added, "There is one female victim hospitalized."

"Ok. I am going to need a *real* cup of coffee right now. Monroe, you're with me. Smythe, you still drinking that froufrou latte crap?"

Chief knew the only way to get any of the nitty gritty was after a Starbucks, and off site so that Monroe could give his 'honest opinion' of what was really going down. Nine times outta ten these cases resolved themselves or got sent directly over to Campus Police, but the nagging suspicion of a Stanford swimmer involved was not setting well.

"We'll be back in ten. See what you've got in the holding cell, Smythe. Clear it. And get me any report Campus Police took last night on this shit," instructed Orzo.

Keeping the drunks in holding meant potential for parental involvement. Chief wanted no part of that action on this.

Beau and the guys met up at Strada. No one had said a word about what Coach said, why positions were not announced, or the fact that Dewey never showed up to practice.

"K, boys. Where's Dewey?" Beau took the lead. "And what the fuck went down last night after I left? I swear to God, I will kick your asses if I have to go down for some shit those fucking freshman football fucks were up to. Who the fuck ratted to Carter?" Silence.

John, Brian, and Joel were facing Beau. Greg and Jorge flanked him. All but Joel were looking at the ground.

Brian, Joel, and Jorge were in the engine on their runner up eight boat the last three seasons. Edgar recently nudged out Jorge and no one was happy about Coach's decision. Rumor out was that Edgar and some freshman from the track team had been picked up by the cops last night and never returned. No one spoke of it.

Unspoken, although understood was that Football had shown up with a crew at about midnight. Football always stormed in and snagged the ladies of their choice after the rest of the gang had spent a couple hours liquoring them up. Wasn't fair, but implicit at all campus parties. Last night was no different, aside from the red garbs. Red received immediate attention on the streets of Cal, and there was some scuffle about *'giving the red ringers what they came for.'*

"I am not fucking kidding here guys. Give me the fucking brief," Beau demanded.

When there was any sort of scrum amongst the guys, a brief was mutually decided upon and sent via Groupme. Stories had to be straight. Beau hadn't seen a brief, or any text at all from the night before.

"Fuckin ay man. I am not gonna sit here and take this shit up the ass. Coach asks me if I am at a party and not one of you can give me the fucking brief? What the actual fuck." Beau was losing his cool.

"Chill the fuck out, Bow. The police shut us down about two but nothing happened." Joel was first to speak. "It was a great party man. Fucking Stanford swim team had their annual scavenger hunt so the red dresses were on point."

Brian mumbled half a recollection of one of the reds being stripped naked and taken out back to 'mattressland.' Something about a hat? According to Brian, she went back there of her own free will and then things got a bit outta hand. Someone had called an ambulance before even calling the cops.

No one in this bunch dared share skin on those mattresses. It was often times freshman or Oaklandiers high on meth party crashing with no idea how foul those things were. If someone from football took a red out back, none of these guys wanted anything to do with it.

"Edgar. Where the fuck is Edgar today, too?" barked Beau.

Unofficially presumed by the group, Edgar Munoz was still in the tank at BPD. No one spoke of it.

John

John sat in silence thinking back on that red dress he'd tossed in to Frankie on

Dewey's bed. *Shit. That probs was not her dress*. He slid his cell out of his backpack and texted Dewey for the third time. Still no reply from his first two texts. WTF. CMB Asshole, he typed.

The doggy in the hallway had been John. He knew he'd been seen by a few passersby but Frankie was begging for it. It wasn't he who had 'taken her up' to begin with, and his pass to Dewey all but wiped him clean of care-taking from that point on. He had taken his turn on two and passed Frankie along, naked and unresponsive—that part he wasn't too proud of.

Shhht. It's not like I even got much of a turn after she kinda went limp on me. He remembered having to hold her up, keep it in, *and* fake install a condom at one point before entry. When he'd seen her this morning, he'd assumed the dress outside of Dewey's door was hers, but now realized his error. *How did a red one make it to three? Fuckin wild night.*

Dewey

Dewey could not give a *shit* about being on time to the damn workouts. No chance he'd be in a boat this season having put on nearly forty, maybe forty-five pounds over the summer. Fuck that legacy shit. He had babes to roll.

Naked tail in his room and an early morning boner— decisions, decisions. For just a second it looked like she was gonna bail, but as quickly as she'd turned her head to say good morning, she'd fallen back against the head board and was back to sleep.

Sleeping Beauty. Shall I kiss and wake you, or delight you with my magic stick? As he fondled her naked breasts, absolutely no push back from her, he was near ejaculation without penetration when the red silk flew at him from the doorway.

Shit. Whoa. Is that—silky smooth and snap—fabric in his left hand, penis in his right. Oh hell, it's coming—the red fabric took to a deep black tone where his stuff splattered the surface. *Hope it's not dry clean only.*

He tried to wipe most of the fluid off the dress before pulling it on over Frankie's heavy head. *Sheesh. For a girl she sure has a boulder for a head.* Once that was done he was able to get both arms through what he figured were arm holes, but damn, was this thing on backwards? *Her problem, not mine. What a night. What a day.* He was king of the world.

Dewey fell back on to his side of the double and decided just a quick couple o' zzz's. "*Life is good. Hell, life is grand,*" he yelled out loud, before he was out.

Getting lots of sleep was important to good health as his mother always said, 'let the boy sleep.'

Upper classmen lived on the second and third floors of the barge. You moved up a floor every year til senior year in the penthouse. Most guys only stayed a year or two but Dewey was a fifth year senior and was tops in location and noise-free quarters two years running. Most visitors didn't even know there was a third floor as those rooms were all off the back of the main house over the parking garage. Peace and quiet, no clanging dishes, or comings and goings. This is the likely reason that no one spotted him or Frankie in the goings on.

Police had shut down the party at about two. John, who had obtained a flaccid Frankie from Edgar a bit earlier, had passed Frankie up the back stairs just before that. Dewey was not about to trudge down and help out with the cleanup. That's what freshmen were for. I got me a naked lady. He had potato-sack carried her to his fortress of fun for some good lovin.

Frankie & Dewey

When Frankie had come to for the second time in Dewey's room, the place was such a pigsty she focused all of her energy on getting the hell out of there. That smell. Two flights of stairs was no small feat, and when she reached the front porch of the house, she rested briefly on the familiar brown couch. Somehow her phone was in her hand, but that was it. Where was her ID wristlet? *Damn. My key.* She scolded herself for being so stupid for taking it off her wrist. *Did I take it off? Did Edgar have it?*

Wait. What happened with Edgar last night? She sort of started to feel like she may have dragged him off the dance floor and begged him to show her his room. A slight memory that they'd shared a blue colored drink and a pink pill earlier on the dance floor but she had no recollection of why or when. *Was it before or after she'd blown Beau all to hell*?

Wait. Where was Beau? Damn, I do not feel good. Frankie threw up on the brown couch. Careful not to get any on herself. *Wait. What the fuck am I doing in a red fucking dress? Shit. I gotta get home. Just a block over to Dwight—or was it two blocks?* She stumbled down the stairs and took a minute on the front lawn to collect herself. She was tangled in a piece of yellow plastic of some kind. "Jesus. Keep the streamers inside you idiots," she slurred out loud. *Just down College, not far at all.*

She was nearly across College when she heard honking and cussing, "Get the fug out the way bitch." *Nasty fucker.*

"Get a job," she hollered back, blazing the bird at him.

Two onlookers whispered to each other. "Shit looks real bad," they agreed louder.

BPD

Back at the precinct, an active Friday morning briefing alerted those just in on the day shift to what happened the night before.

Monroe began. "We have a possible 243 with witnesses; drunk and disorderly at that boat house on Bancroft. Another incident of possible 240, complicated by female students from across the bay. Initially requested back-up by Campus police. Request denied due to the violent nature of the assault, with witnesses present. Also complicated by the fact that rival school activities breaching a code, having something to do with the athlete code of conduct. Victim 1 is at Berkeley medical center with multiple contusions and refusing a rape kit." This shit was exasperating. Same shit, different day as far as the police could tell.

PC 243 was a sexual assault. PC 240 was a violent crime and possible sexual assault. The stories were getting muddied by the possibility there were, in fact, two violent assaults at the party; but the police were not yet in on that scoop.

"Some discussion of a harassment and violation of personal rights on private property. Couple of the frat boys lawyered up rather than give us a statement." Jones was patrol interviewing at the frat after clearing the place. "These fucking frats," he added. "We have two in the tank." Referring to Munoz, and freshman track and fielder, Andre Flint.

"The ladies could not agree on the nature of the offense against their gal who was hospitalized but they were yappin about discrimination, racial retaliation, and protection for witnesses if they were to testify. These kids were genuinely stoned outta their minds spewing legal and talking about calling their daddy's attorneys—long night." Tazey sighed.

"Chief, if I may interject," from the back of the room Officer Renee Blotto had something she wanted to say. "I have spent nearly five hours with Victim 1, doctors, nurses, and a couple other witnesses. It looks like we have tears in the vaginal area, bruising over most of victim 1's body, stitches required in the head and neck regions—a very violent attack, sir—in addition to the SA. Physicians pleaded with her to further examine but she was in too much pain for the internal examination. Victim 1 is sedated and requesting no further interview questions. It really looks like we will not get any charges moving forward from her. She did, however, give me quite a story about a potential victim who 'had it worse' according to multiple accounts. Both Victim 1 and her friends told of a white female victim, unconscious, being repeatedly violated by multiple assailants. I'd like permission to take Monroe back with me to the Barge, I mean house, this morning to see if by chance there are other victims."

"Absolutely not Blotto. Let's stick with the three characters we already have. Another one comes forward, maybe we get lucky and she reports to campus police. We do not go digging for bodies, am I clear?" Exasperated by what he was hearing, Chief stormed out without listening to the rest of the briefing.

"Nancy, I'm gonna need a Starbucks—strong—and large." Orzo dropped a twenty on the desk and shut his door behind him. Two in one day could make for a serious flare up, but his headache craved caffeine.

"That'd be a venti, sir. Right away." Nancy stood up to go get to it. "Nope. No Monroe. I would not advise it..."

Monroe strode past, opened and shut the door to the office and with that Nancy grabbed her bag and decided they are big boys, let them sort it out. *I need a latte.*

The barge had been taped off at about 2:30 am. By morning, rumors were flying around campus. Many had seen the red dress gang before and after—'was one hospitalized or did she die'—questioned two passersby. "I saw two reds at Strada earlier, walkin shameless," said another.

"Betches wearin red had better beware." Two girls laughed.

"You think it's an actual crime scene investigation?" inquired another.

"CSI Berkeley, ladies and gentlemen, tonight on 20/20." ENGINerd blazoned across the two boys' matching navy tees.

Everyone passing along on Piedmont had a comment and jab.

Plenty of frat parties got outta hand. Numerous police and fire trucks frequented the Piedmont /College /Bancroft /Haste blocks on weekend nights. The yellow tape at ten am on a Friday morning, that was newsworthy.

"Do you smell that?" asked one gal to another. "I think I smell smoke?"

"Just the usual stench at this corner on the weekends," one assured the other.

Berkeley Athletic Department

"We are shutting it down," bellowed Willard. "Get me that asshole in charge of frats. What the hell is his name?"

The athletics department early Friday morning is in cover-up mode. Department playbook is clear; shovel the shit onto the frat plate *ASAP*. Greek life on campus is in the addendums; get the issue *out* of athletics.

"Andrea, do we have word back yet about that Barge? Is it a sanctioned fraternity or not?" barks Willard. "This is not a drill folks. I just hung up with a doctor from the Tang. They have a walk-in but Berkeley Medical Center got an ambulance transfer last night... from...that...God... damned...barge."

"Sheila. We are gonna need legal in the conference room ay sap."

"Yes sir. They have been contacted," replied Sheila. "They wondered about police involvement, sir. Is it campus or city?"

"Fuck if I know," he roared, as he strode through the development desk area. "We gotta shut this shit down and fast. I got a bunch a fuckin alum donors here tonight and tomorrow for the Oregon game. I ain't got time for this shit." he slammed his door. "RTFM," he hollered at the door.

Inside the hospital room, a raised voices dispute about whether or not the girls would be pressing charges.

"Fuck this. All we did was hit a fucking party. No one asked for any of this to happen. How about these assholes *stop raping us*? Saying we should stay away from a certain frat or party is like saying it's *our fault* for bein' alive."

"First, we don't know if the guy was a frat boy or not. So blaming Greek life partying for some fucking boater douche's actions makes no sense at all. Second, we will damn well go wherever we please and should not have to think twice about whether or not some guy is going to rape us. Instead of blaming us for going to

73

some fucking party, how about you grow a pair and join a fucking antisex crime campaign or some shit." Red dress number two was letting the intern have it with gusto.

"You come at us like 'not saying she deserved it *but* she was at a frat' is *stupid as fuck*." red dress number three added. "This is some bullshit. Somehow we are to blame for Jessie getting fucked up royal."

"Not tryna say you're an idiot doc, like at all, but there are certain offensive things you shouldn't be sayin right now dude, and this was one of them." Two chimed back. "No fucking way we leave here without an attorney. They gotta see this shit. I called my dad...and I got pictures."

"All I am trying to explain to you ladies is, *if* your friend Jessie wakes up and wants to press charges, you are going to have to give me a name of who did this," mollified the doctor on call. "We need her okay to do the internal exam, and we need a name to give to the police. I'll be back in an hour or so."

Berkeley Police Officer Renee Blotto

Blotto was enraged. "We know there has to be another suspect involved, Monroe. Those gals went on and on about some girl getting it worse, and there being more than a dozen on-lookers to some sort of gang bang. All witnesses agreed there was some sumo-wrestling-sized white guy there, and a brunette being passed from guy to guy. All we got in the tank is a mid to small build Hispanic and his scared for his life twiggy track buddy.

Two guys too small to have been instigators in my opinion."

"Look, Renee, I'll see what I can get out of the kid in the tank, that's the best I can do. Crossing the Chief on shit like this is not a good idea—for what, some sorority girl who had one too many and won't remember a thing about it," he rallied. "We are not riding our first rodeo; another day, another *possible* sexual assault. Get at me when someone wants to press charges, or name names."

"IDing the white guy at over 250 pounds is not going to take rocket science. Someone at that house saw something, we just need to go back." Blotto could not let it go. She continued lobbying Detective Tazey until he finally agreed.

"Take someone from patrol on day shift; a fresh set of eyes. The tape needs to come down from the perimeter— and if someone *offers up* new information, take it. But don't say I said so. Just troll the joint like it's SOP, got it?"

"Standard operating procedure, got it." Blotto hit the hall with a bit of a rush. "Woops, sorry Smythe." She bumped into the detective as she came out of the conference room; he headed in, she out.

"Where's the fire?" inquired Smythe, but Blotto was off.

Dewey was making his way to the kitchen when he noticed the yellow tape out front on the lawn. *What the fuck?*

"Hey man, you talk to the cops last night?"

Nosey little cleaning crew we got today. Cops? *WTF. I never heard any cops.* He strode into the dining room with the vigor of a famished warrior seeking a roasted hog. What time was it? Fucking missed breakfast and no lunch buffet out yet. Cereal; breakfast of champions, always on tap. Dewey went into the kitchen for a baking bowl. *Damn cereal bowls don't hold shit.*

Out the porch window he thought he spotted a couple of Blue's trolling. He approached and opened the screen door off the back. "Hey, hunting Easter eggs a bit early aren'tcha?" he laughed at his own hilarity.

Blotto looked at her ride along partner Officer Jones.
Jones nodded.

Back at BPD

"So, let's review. We have a couple of skins in the tank, one victim hospitalized, about twelve interviewees but a couple of POI's I told Chief I want to find. That big guy we've met before, Beau, they call him. Beauregard Pierce, big ass douchebag but always able to slither out of the sling—his name pops up on the regular at that Barge dump. No idea about the alleged female victim but she's a POI; at least ten people admit to witnessing some pretty gnarly shit being done to her ass—literally."

Monroe and Smythe are back at the white board.

"Get patrol to bring in this guy Pierce." Monroe expects Smythe to task manage while he strategizes.

"Think we're gonna need another board," replies Smythe. "Martha, can we get another easel and board please," he hollers across the way to assistant Martha. He actually enjoys his role as a 'doer.'

"Already ordered from the basement," she is quick to reply. "Anybody in there want to order a pizza for lunch today?" They all nod in agreement that it is going to be a long one.

Blotto and Jones get very little out of Dewey. He's hungry he says, and they 'don't have a warrant,' he beams with pride at his smarts. Jones takes the lead and tries for a bro moment.

"So man, looks like it was a great party last night, plenty 'o red cups on the lawn is a sure sign things were hoppin," starts Jones.

"Yeah, well it wasn't just red cups your man was working.

I happen to have got me a red dressed date last night as well." Dewey does need to brag about this to someone.

"Date?" probes Jones.

"Sleep over date," replies Dewey. "I'll have to tell you all about it another time though, like when you have a warrant." Chuckling, he reenters the back door. "Sayonara Suits."

Blotto is feverishly taking notes. Red dress, date, sleep over.

"Jones. We gotta get back in that house." She is more determined now.

"Agreed," replies Jones. "But not without a warrant. Jeez, what a smart ass."

"We need a name." Blotto is up the stairs to the door. "Excuse me, sir, can I just get your name for our SOP." Acronyms almost always confuse the drunks into compliance.

Hmm? Must be some sort of box they gotta check off they came by and all..."Bryce," he bellows. "Bryce Howard Dewey, the third." *Making pops proud today folks.*

"And your *date*, what was her name?" she prodded.

"Fra— Wait. What...uhm. The lass is *actually* my buddy's best gal. I can't be goin all rogue and namin' names. You get that warrant and ya'll come back now ya hear?"

Beau

Beau spent an hour texting and probing with John outside of Strada. The others left without even ordering, knowing full well no good would come out of lingering. No one was talking. From what they could gather, police detained Edgar Munoz and some freshman caught in the wrong place at the wrong time. John agreed to head over to the Barge and do some asking around.

"My bad Beau. I hit the head then back to my place after my sneak attack in the stairwell. Man, I got nothing for ya."

"Sneak what?" Beau was pissed. They'd been seated nearly an hour and as John gets up to leave, he mentions a hit?

"Dude. After you left, Frankie came on to Edgar in a big way. I didn't wanna tell you man, cause hell I figured you were done with her and that's why you left." John sat back down.

"Edgar passed her up my way with some shit about not letting up, she kept singing 'more, more, more' like she was some fuckin 70s rock star or some shit. Hell, I could barely hold her up but she had me like 'back in black' and shit. She starts blowin' me right there in the hallway so I spun her around and gave it to her."

Holy shit. Frankie gettin *caught in the washer* as they like to say about a girl on spin cycle. He'd seen and heard and all but never actually *knew* the chicks gettin hit like that.

Rumor was Oakland bitches lookin' to get pounded showed up high on crack regularly. Hell last season, he'd had a shot at some black girl who assured the guys she wasn't askin' for call backs just looking to get some, but he'd chickened out. Something clanging in his head from Brandy about sex meaning something and being the only sex worth having.

John stayed another minute or two and shared the spin story with Beau. Sounded like she begged Edgar, or a coupla guys, before being passed off to Dewey on his way up to three.

"All clean before midnight." He swore he barely had any alcohol so Coach had freakin nothing to complain about.

The other shit was some football boys spinning a red dress out back. Something about how the gang had to block the kitchen because the girls' friends didn't think she should be doin things on accounta they were messed up on some strange herbs or some shit. John had very little in the way of details.

"Talk to football man—some muscling up of a few reds. Four or five guys getting a little rough with one chick in the yard. Honestly, I didn't see anything out of the ordinary last night dude," he explained to Beau.

"Listen. Let me get over there and see what went down with Edgar, cause he and Dewey never showed up to tryouts." John was on foot and left Beau deep in thought.

Mother Fucker. I leave that bitch for ten minutes and she dips on me to the dance floor. Take her up to the toilet cause she says she has to pee, and fuckin ay all I get is a blow. Damn straight I was done with her. AM DONE WITH HER. These fuckin college girls don't know shit about being a decent girlfriend for fuck sake.

Interrogation Room at BPD

"So, Edgar. Your statement is that the woman you had sex with was consensual?"

"Yessir." Trying for one word answers. Edgar wonders if he shouldn't give a bit more detail to be believable. *Frankie begged me. Would not take no for an answer. Practically assaulted me. Prob not gonna fly. Will keep that to myself.*

"And this woman was known to you prior to last evening's soiree?"

"Yessir."

"But you don't know her name other than what you all call her? Frankie."

"Yessir."

"Say we put you in a line up along with a few buddies for the Stanford student victimized at the party. She won't point to you?"

"No, sir. No. Mine was wearing black. The Stanford Slu— ladies wore red sir."

"So. You did, in fact, see a few ladies from across the bay now?" *Interrogations can twist and turn until you finally get the information you need.* Detective Monroe knew he was on to something.

"Uhm. Yes. Some red." Confusing himself as to what he'd already let slip.

"When you say red. Can you describe any of these young ladies for us son?"

"No, sir." *Shut the fuck up E.*

Interrogations went on through the early morning hours on Friday and both Edgar and his wimpy buddy seemed to be genuinely scared of their own shadows. Hardly man enough to batter and bruise up a few strong female athletes travelling in a group.

"Chief. I don't think I can see either of these two hitting or attacking a girl. Hell, they look like a coupla fruity lovers, if you ask me."

Edgar had spent a fair amount of time when 'no one was looking' schooling Andre and holding his hands reassuring him they'd be out in no time.

"We didn't do nothin wrong brotha, they can't keep us here. Just keep your mouth shut and answer the questions with yes or no. We good."

Andre hated it when spicks and white boys tried to go all 'brotha' on him. *This stupid fuck was not his brother.* Five hours felt like fifty by now.

"Deny until you die. Well, not really die." Edgar would not shut up. Andre knew this shit was being taped and watched from behind that mirror.

"Those ladies are muscular, sir, and they described the gang that took them on as a bunch of 'fat fucks high on something strange.' If these two got their socks wet in a stream, they'd be crying to their mommas," continued the detective.

"Okay, Edgar," came a voice over the boys in the holding room. "Say we put you in a line–up. The young lady over at the medical center will not point to you?"

"No, sir." Edgar wondered about the Wizard of Oz movie just then and how the voice sounded the same...

"Andre?"

"Sir. I didn't touch no young ladies last night, I swear. Didn't touch none." Andre was quick to reply and sounded sincere; almost as though he was about to burst into tears.

"You two are free to go," came the Oz-like voice again. *Go where?* No door handle they could see to even try to run for it.

Moments later, the wall opened, and a pocked-faced officer led the two down the hall and out to the front lobby of the station. "You got your phones and particulars in that envelope there." He pointed to a large manila envelope Edgar held tight to. "I might suggest you Uber or Lyft it. You two look like hell," he added.

FRIDAY 2:15 PM, UC AD CONFERENCE ROOM

Seated in the conference room were coaches from Cal boating, football, basketball, and track and field. Someone must have heard something about last night in this bunch.

"Carr. Where's Carter?" bellowed Willard. "Get him in here. We are not starting without him."

"Uh...he says I'm in charge. He and Janine packed up the kids and headed—well, I think maybe he might be taking a few days..."

Carr was both excited and horrified that Carter had left him in charge. He'd been assistant on a number of Pac 12 rows and this was his year—move a couple bodies around.

"NOW." shouted Willard. Carr jumped to his feet in alarm. He instinctively left the room but stood in the hallway knowing full well there was no 'getting Carter' to be done. He decided to hit the toilet and give Willard a moment to cool down.

"Thank you all for coming," started Willard in a sing song tone. *These people need to be outta here by 3, 3:15 at the latest.*

"Don't thank me, sir." From the back of the room, a large black man stood and bellowed. "My name is Howard Render. Attorney representing Ms. Jessica Tucker, who is currently undergoing medical treatment and evaluation at BMC. An obvious victim of sexual assault on your campus Thursday evening between the hours of eleven pm and midnight. It is clear and apparent the University of California at Berkeley has *repeatedly and deliberately* ignored known harassment and assaults on campus at the corner of Piedmont and Bancroft; a dwelling known to many current and former students—uh victims, as 'The Barge.' Sir. I plan to take this case under Title IX with Ms. Tucker and wonder if maybe you might like to speak to me in your office. Privately."

Willard took a long breath before calmly turning to Andrea with his reply. "Andrea, kindly escort Mr. Render to the front office to make an appointment in my office, *privately*, sometime next week." He looked back to Render and nodded. *Take that. Fucking scumbag lawyers all up in here on the sneak."*

Andrea was careful not to show any reaction at all to what just transpired. With a graceful smile she said, "Of course sir." She opened the door and waited while Render slid his notebook and cell phone into his bag and exited.

"Coaches; Phil, Max, Herb, let's begin again. Thank you all for coming." Willard appeared unshaken and with resolve addressing the guests he had expected. *This ain't my first rodeo. I damn sure am not talking to any mo-fo lawyers—that's what we got the three amigos over there for.* His eyes stopped on Phil, Max, and Herb each individually before he continued.

Carr had slipped back into his seat during a commotion of some kind where a big unknown dude in a suit was escorted out by Willard's assistant director Andrea.

"Now then. What've we got?" The meeting lasted until nearly five. Three solid hours of defensive planning amongst the Cal staff and coaches. Play books are crisp and clear among the athletic staffers.

1. Boaters would refrain from attending the next athlete's mixer.

2. Coaches would counsel their respective players on therules of NCAA; namely remind all team members the dangers of possessing or using alcohol, serving potential under-agers, engaging in illegal or unethical conduct or behaviors; all means

for losing scholarship dollars and potentially being removed from team.

3. Legal would take the matter up with the heads of theGreek society in shutting down the house in question.

4. This issue will be dealt with in-house; no one speaks to media or other outside source on the matter. A standard reply of, *'there is nothing to see here.'*

5. Don't let a one-time incident become a two week story.

"...and folks, let me remind those of you in this room. Stanford will always be tryna get at us for somethin; let's not allow this to affect the big game and our alumni weekend—which begins right now at our tailgate you're all invited to at both Gattis and Goldman terraces. Go Bears." With that, Willard walked out. *I need a stiff one.*

Beau

Beau was beginning to get a major head ache. Head to the library to meet the tutor, or crash for an hour before pizza and beer with the guys; Friday tradition. *I'm beat.* Fuck Coach Carter if he thinks he can spin some sort of rule bustin' on me. Football assistants have been after me since sophomore year, and they get way better gear. A power nap is just what the Bowman needed right now.

Police Department

"Monroe. Whadda we got over at in-house lock up that looks like they can pass for college dummies?" Chief inquired.

"You think we're gonna need it, Chief? I think maybe we got enough witnesses we can ID this Frankie and Beau pair. They come up in just about everyone's account at some point or another," stated Detective Monroe. "Pretty sure Bowman is one Beauregard Francis Pierce; I sent patrol to bring him in for questioning already."

Friday PM

Holly

Holly is on the porch at 2756 Benvenue before ten. No answer. Maybe the bell doesn't work, she thinks to herself, grabbing her keys, she knocks on the window. Where did she learn that—someone told her window and key knock noise travels further. After about three minutes, she's almost to the corner but something makes her turn around. Was that someone looking out the window? She has an eerie feeling. It's getting dark and she picks up the pace back to her place.

Her √ text goes out to Haley at 10:07pm. Home safe. Tired, she decides to read a chapter in stats, that'll put her right out. Just something sweet before bed, maybe I need an Almond Joy.

Frankie

"Who the fuck is that blonde bitch?" asks Frankie out loud, to no one. *Where have I seen her before*? A nagging voice internalizes.

Frankie is between the toilet and her mini-fridge a couple of times before determining it's gonna need a ginger ale and soda crackers run to Derby; if she is gonna live through this nightmare. She's pulled on sweats and tee shirt when she hears the doorbell. Not. In. The. Mood. She watches out her front window until the coast is clear, then heads down and out.

Missing practice was something she'll deal with later. Getting to Derby and back without seeing any one was the current agenda item. *Fuck. What a shit feeling.* Weak and blurred, but starving and determined. *No one can see me like this.*

"Crap," she says out loud. She's forgotten her phone. No energy to go back up, and no need to talk to anyone. Uber, text, or GPS it to Derby and back. No phone, no problem. She's got a $20 on her and won't need ID for crackers and pop.

Where the hell is my ID wristlet anyways? "Fuck." *I sure hope no one else in the house comes back and locks me out.* "Key gone along with ID," she grumbles. *Damn. Did I leave the door unlocked?* Her body aches like the devil; *get*

Advil, too.

Beau

Un-Fucking-Believeable. *I put the sock out. Who the fuck is knocking on my damn door wakin' my ass up?* "Go away," he shouted.

The knocking got louder. Sorta out of hand even. *WTF.* "Tryna break down my fuckin door, asshole?" Beau was spewing to a blue before his eyes and brain could catch up with his words. "Uhm. Sorry officers. Can I help you?" "Beauregard Francis Pierce?" Patrol one asked.

"Fuck." Beau tried to shut the door on them but patrol two had his boot to the thing solid as a rock.

"Not so fast kid," he said with a smile. "We just wanna ask you a few questions. Come down to the station with us nice-like and you'll be back to your beauty sleep before midnight." He mocked.

"Fuck Me."

"Watch the language son." Patrol one. "Let's go."

"Lemme get my shoes on. Fuck. How long's this gonna take?" asked Beau with a bit more even tone.

"Now that depends on you, doesn't it kid." Again mocking from patrol number two.

Derby Market

"Frankie P. What up gurl? I hadn't seen yo ass since…" Jeremy Reynolds stammered. "Yo gurl, you aight?"

Of course. Sacks being directly adjacent to Derby Frankie had crossed paths with none other than her 'freshman-forgetaboutit' douche bag boyfriend of six days.

Not even a week as FBO, Jeremy appeared outta nowhere time and again, like a bad habit year after year.

"Hey J." she ducked her head quickly. She'd only looked in the mirror once intentionally since last night. As she'd feared, swelling and redness had become a full on black eye on the left side.

"Yo gurl, no joke. You ok?" Jeremey queried her and grabbed for her arm. With cat like reflexes, she slapped his hand away and grimaced. Every part of her body ached. "K, bitch. Be like that. See if I ever spot you a latte again. Damn."

Thank God he'd gone away without much more than an ugly look. *I have got to*—BOOM. Just like that Frankie vomited on the sidewalk in front of the salon. It was closed, thank God. She scooted into Derby market wiping her mouth on her sleeve.

Frankie never did make it back with the ginger ale or crackers. She got one foot in the door to Derby and collapsed on the floor. The grimy, filthy—not in six or seven years has it seen any bleach related solvent— concrete floor of the Derby Market.

Holly could not believe her eyes; same girl, same limp state of being, same day even but alas a different outfit.

"I call the police," shouted the register attendant. "Or the ambulance 911."

"I'm ok. I'm good." Frankie was in a seated position in the blink of an eye.

"My name is Holly. What's yours?" Holly was breathing erratically. Adrenaline rushing through her body. *Why do I feel so weird? I don't even know this person.*

"None of your business," replied Frankie curtly. Admittedly, she was having some trouble today. *No one...no one can see me like this.*

"Look. My name is Holly. I picked you up in the middle of the street earlier today. You do not have to tell me your name but you must let me help you up. You have some sort of—well, you seem to be—you just don't look 'okay' to the store manager. Unless you let me help you, he's totally calling the cops," she politely explained. *Why oh why, again, did I get myself into this? Candy bars after ten o'clock at night was never a good idea.*

Frankie was having difficulty processing. *Earlier? Cops? WTF.*

It took some convincing, and a hell of a lot of assistance in righting her, but Holly grabbed two candy bars, paid the clerk, and walked Frankie back to her place like a human crutch. The two were seated on Holly's futon couch. Unwrapping the bar and passing half to Frankie. Holly tried breathing exercises, before trying to speak.

"I hate nuts," spewed Frankie.

"Eat around it or spit it out. Does not matter to me," was Holly's reply. "You have got to eat something." Up and to the pantry she went, grabbing for an old package of stale graham crackers, she plated them for her guest of honor. A glass of water next to the plate on the coffee table, and Frankie was horizontal before she got back.

"Look. I appreciate your hospitality and all, but I really am beat. Mind if I just lay here a minute or two? Then I am out."

Much like earlier in the day; a very frank and matter-offact tone from someone who cannot walk.

She left the room and texted her mother. Even at 1 or 2 am back home, her mom always heard the buzz and answered her calls.

Police Dept

At the station before 5, it was looking like Monroe would be staying late again. "You talked to him last winter." lobbied the evening shift detective Mark Tazey. "And if I miss date night tonight, Trixey will leave me."

Nearly an hour later, and they were no closer to solidifying a case against Beau in the issue of the swimmer banged up at the barge.

Beau

"I was out of there by eleven. Don't have any idea what Frankie's fucking last name is, and never saw even one red dress on my way out." He'd been pretty clean with his version of events even after being asked eleven different ways.

"Yes, I have a girlfriend. No she doesn't go to Cal. And no I did not '*go to or leave with*' *anyone* last night. I was there less than an hour tops." Explained Beau. "One drink. I had *one drink* but not enough to blow or any shit like that— plus I fuckin walked. So what's the crime you tryna pin on me?"

He was exasperated with the questioning, his mind wandering back to when and where he last spotted Frankie. *She was dancing WITH EDGAR. That bastard. I will fucking kill him.*

Dewey

Dewey was questioned by patrol and left at the Barge. "Fuckin ay, looks like I missed quite a party out back," he said to the cleaning lady at the sink. *Fuck. She don't speak English.* He stumbled back to the dining cereal supply. *Fuckin sex fuckin makes a man hungry.*

93

Deep into his second bowl of fruity pebbles. His brain was whirling. *It's fuckin Friday night, sir. I need to get myself cleaned up and ready for the dance floor at Kaps.*

Grabbing his cell out of the waistband of his thread-bare champion gym shorts, he texted Beau.

'Boys Night at Ladies Night at Kaps. You in?' No reply.

Beau

Beau was dropped back at his place about 7:30; too late for the free happy hour slices, but starving nonetheless. Dominoes delivery was fuckin outrageous in Cali so he grabbed a frozen Tony's and stuck it in the cold oven. 425 degrees was gonna take a few, so he ate an unrecognizable hoagie of some kind; belonging to who knows, having been in the fridge for nearly a month. All against his better judgment but he was effing starving. *God damn that was shit. How much longer for the fucking pizza? Fuck.* He never set the timer. *Whatever. I'm fucking starving.* He bellied up to the TV with a blackened crusted, lukewarm in the middle, pepperoni delight. *Tastes better than that shit.*

Police questions. Coach up in his grill. This day could not get any worse. Tosh 2.0, fuck yeah.

He fell back against the couch and sunk in with the entire pizza. Benefit of eating alone, you don't even need to cut the damn thing. Wiping his hands on his sweats, he noticed an odd smear of what looked like blood on the other thigh. Must be sauce. Shit gets everywhere.

The back of his brain tingled with some recognition of this red substance, which was probably *not* pizza sauce on his leg. *What was it? Did something happen last night?* He went back to eating his pizza, spot forgotten.

Girl Talk

Holly and Frankie talked til nearly 3am. Once she'd worked past the hard outer shell, Holly began to see a frightened young woman inside. A girl probably much like she herself just a few years back; naïve and curious, arriving on the sprawling campus having googled Sproul Plaza and watching 'Berkeley in the 60's' with her folks. *But wait. Did she say she was a senior?*

With little or no recollection of the night prior, Frankie pressed Holly over and over about who she saw when, at what time, on what floor. How many red dresses? Most importantly. How Holly surmised she'd ended up tangled in red D&G.

"Sure makes sense as to why you were hangin' outta that dress so dangerously. It was three sizes too small for anyone over the age of ten," deduced Holly. "On backwards at that." A slight giggle on Frankie's face finally.

They'd confirmed they had both stayed clear of the trash bucket of punch, but there was a slight recollection that nagged at Frankie. Had she consumed a bit of something on the dance floor? Was someone passing pills? And if yes, what did she wash it down with? Frankie had heard that kids pop pills. Advil, Adderall—whatever—without water, but she herself had a horrible gag reflex and needed to be equipped with a liquid before swallowing any pill at all.

"What even *is* Molly Water?" asked Holly. Neither of them were really sure.

Both girls danced gently around the elephant in the room. Frankie was bruised up, in lots of pain, and genuinely concerned about the possibility of having had unprotected sex last night. From the pain in her lower area, something pretty intense had transpired. Being an athlete and in good physical condition, they'd both agreed, was how she was able to 'walk away' from the grim setting earlier.

She was lost in thought too about her and Beau. *Were they now an item? Would she soon be FBO with a Cal Boater? Why oh why did her asshole hurt so badly?*

"You were hardly walking." pointed out Holly.

"Oh I walked," argued Frankie. "Walked right home as soon as I...well, maybe you and that guy—look, I'm alive right?"

The decided they both needed a good night's sleep. Frankie too bushed to make it home accepted a pillow and blanket from Holly. *Sheesh. She uses Downey too, such a MOM.* The scent dropped her quickly into a deep sleep in no time. Holly sent another √ text to her little sis. Warm loving thoughts of home were also tied to those checkmark texts. That little bit of connection. California had the same blue sky and sunshine, but none of the cozy warmth of her family and ministry in Florida.

As Holly pulled up her comforter just below her chin she looked up to the now darkened ceiling and said out loud, "Thank you lord. I know that you will never give me more than I can handle, but today was quite the test. I love you. You are my shepherd, I am your servant. Goodnight and God Bless."

Longing for the comfort of Mom's meatloaf and her sister's warm embrace—the spooning and giggling into the night about when they'd actually be bedding with a boy. Sister Hayley would sneak into Holly's room many nights just because.

Senior year, Holly's parents had upgraded the bed in her room to a queen. "Well honey, to be perfectly honest with you, when you leave for college we'll be using you room as our formal guest room. Be sure to pack up a mementos box because we'll be re-decorating as well. Teal is just not a 'welcome guests' kinda color." She'd flatly reported.

John

John was eyed by officers just outside the barge as he walked right on by. Yellow tape and a patrol car. *I ain't checkin in on Dewey while this shit's goin down.* He walked off in the opposite direction.

John prided himself on being one of the few boaters on the squad with any common sense. Take a turn with her ONLY after the bitch has consented and is creamed up nicely by another—pass her on to someone who will undoubtedly have final fingerprints on 'er, then get the fuck outta there. This final set o' hands also charged with getting her into the Uber/Lyft.

Fuck. He was so smart he didn't even *have* the Uber app. Anytime the boys brought up the need for wheels he'd been sure to remind them all he couldn't help with calling for the ride, but he'd *Venmo* his $5 for the tip. $5 for a 5, as the saying goes.

"Fly above the fray." Like his father had taught him. Along with, 'Deny until you die.' *Words to live by. My fucking dad is...the...shit.*

Jessie woke up to her mother in tears by her bedside. *Where the fuck...who...what...was she...HOSPITAL?*

"Mom. I'm fine." she assured her. "Please, please, please stop."

How many times had she said those words to her mother all through high school; and then moving all the way from Monterey to campus 40 miles east? This felt different. And this was pretty fucking surreal. *What the hell happened last night?*

"Oh sweetheart." The flood gate opened and Jessie's hysterical mother was shuffled into the hall by Harper.

"Dad, really. I just want to be alone." She'd never seen her ever-tan, Polo stylish, country club father look so ashen. *WTF. Harper. Get back in here. I gotta get this story straight.*

Without words, he touched her hand and followed her mother out the door. *This was all his fault, he NEVER should have agreed to her joining that slutty sorority. When he was a Stanford man things were entirely different, entirely.*

"Good Morning Jessie. My name is Roberta. I am your day nurse for today. Are you feeling up to eating a little something before we get you up and out for a stroll." Roberta placed a menu on top of the sheet/blanket/sheet set up. *Who? What? A day nurse? How long have I been here?*
Julia, Harper. Where were they?

"Can I pee?" asked Jessie.

"Well. I sure do hope so," joked Roberta. She laughed out loud, but then caught herself when she saw the pathetic look on her patient's face.

"Be sure to position yourself so I can catch a sample in the commode though dear. We need to do some testing." She was back to maternal nurturing voice without a beat.

"Testing for what?" demanded Jessie. "I'm fine." When she tried to raise her head from the pillow she wondered exactly how in the world they had bound her down. Was she super glued to this plastic ass mattress? With all the strength she had she could barely raise to sit up.

Roberta helped her by supporting her back and taking her left arm. "Ouch." Jessie's right arm was in a sling but the left was sore as hell too.

99

"I'm so sorry dear. Let's just start slowly," soothed Roberta.

What the fuck. Why can't I walk? I can't get out of bed. Tears began to roll down Jessie's cheeks. Her brain was sending flashes. She had a slight recollection of following two football players out back to get a ball cap from the trunk of their—she never saw any cars in the lot—a slight visual from her initial reaction to seeing just the basketball nets, a couple of balls, and an entire lot full of 'something.' It had been difficult to get her footing. *Why can't I remember?*

Thinking back

Tradition at the barge was to play a bit of mattress ball before the party got rolling and the mattresses became the 'fortress of fuckin' out back. The entire basketball court / back parking lot was covered in outdoor mattresses. Try dribbling on that whydontcha!?

"Hey. So, we're headed out back for a toque right?"

"Oh. We're gonna give you a torque alright."

"No, seriously. I need a hat—a toque you know—a knit cap."

"Listen, bitch. You come to mattress land, you get what you get and you don't throw a fit."

"Wait. Where?"

Thwack. A quick backhand to the face. Too startled to scream, Jessica felt her arms being pulled together behind her back.

"Bitches show up to Cal dressed in red gotta expect a lesson comin' to em." The big guy put a cotton soaked cloth to her nose and she was out.

Filthy old mattresses were lined up behind the dumpsters between parties for safe keeping. Never ever would the trash crew touch 'em back there. These particular mattresses were collected up any time there was a campus-wide mass move out— at least once annually.

Raul and Andre lowered the limp body to the soft surface just off the back porch. When their eyes met, Raul thought he saw tears welling up on the kid.

"Shake it off man. She knows what the what—showin up here wearing scarlet red—'sides, she won't remember a thing. Let's go."

"Dude. You said you were giving her a hat and shit."

"Fuck off kid. You ain't got no idea what you're talkin about. If you're smart, you'll forget you ever saw this one man."

The streets of Berkeley are riddled with next-to-new mattresses mid-to-late May when leases were up; grads were moving on, or in some cases students were simply moving to a new apartment but didn't have a truck to move the bed. Parents would shell out another $4-500. (IKEA really is such a great deal on mattresses— they're practically disposable.) Who knew how old some of them were. Only once in a while did a homeless guy or gal take it upon themselves to drag one over to People's Park and the boys would have to find a replacement.

"Dude. She's all yours, we out" Raul had made enough deals with enough devils to know you simply deliver the merch then bolt. He took a wad of cash from a pair of lugheads and headed back into the Barge.

Keeping the football cronies in random ass bitches and hoes was starting to cost a bit too much off the top. Time to put them out back and get inside. Back to the money makers.

"Hey, Edgar. Get Andre a drink man, he's all shook up." With that, Raul was off to the next transaction.

Andre That girl Jessica had lay motionless for nearly two hours before Andre got his nerve up to call for an ambulance.

He tried to ease his conscience by helping the other red dresses out with the jockeys and all. What went on out back was just not right.

"I...Hi. Uhh...Hello. I'm calling because I think there's a girl hurt real bad. No. I can't give you my name but I can tell you that she's laying out back of...well, on the corner of Piedmont and Bancroft. Can you just send an ambulance?" he hung up quickly and tossed his phone into his duffle. He took a second to settle his breathing.

Never again. He began packing his things to get moved outta this place for good. It was still nearly a week before he'd have an actual dorm room. *Fuck it. I cannot stay here.*

As he opened his door to leave, duffel over his shoulder, Raul greeted him with a knowing sort of look.

"Where you headed man?" No reply. "Yeah, I think maybe you'd better just turn around and camp the fuck right back where you were soldier!"

He waited while Andre put his bag down, then nodded towards the mattress.

"I think I'll call you Alberto from now on."

Back to Jessica

"It's ok honey, you can do it." Roberta did her best to swing Jessie's legs sideways off the bed. In an instant, nausea overcame her.

"Uh...oh fuck..." projectile vomit hit the wall first and dripped down to the floor nearing Roberta's white shoes. A fair amount of liquid with very little in the way of 'chunks' being she'd basically 'drank her dinner' the night prior.

"You're ok. Let it out...let's just see if we can't put some weight on your feet now dear." *Is she a fucking robot? Did she not just witness a scene right outta Bridesmaids...or The Sand Lot for cripes sake? Projectile...fucking...vom...bitch.*

103

"Are you fucking kidding me? I just barfed. What the fuck." Jessie dropped backwards onto a pillow also assuredly covered in plastic wrap. "Is there a fucking pillow case in this place?" she barked.

Jessica's Friends

Harper and Julia were giving Officer Blotto another description of the gang from the night before down in the lobby.

The Annual Sorority Scavenger Hunt. On the list, year after year, was the coveted Cal Gear obtained from an athlete across the bay. It had to be officially issued Cal gear from a male student athlete, no cheating and grabbing something at the Student Store.

"It doesn't count if you buy 'em, and we don't cheat."

Gang load of football players had arrived late to the party and said they had a toque in their trunk out back. Jessie had followed and would be right back.

"It was like divide and conquer." *'You two get the Jockeys, I'll get the toque and meet you out front. This place smells like sewage.'* "It really stunk bad in there."

She had assured them she was fine and they booked up the stairs to steal a pair of Jockey brand men's underwear; had to be Jockey.

They had an easy time of it with the undies. Some wimpy kid escorted them up, dug into a duffle bag, and produced two pair — one Jockey, one Hanes.

"We took them both just in case we'd get extra credit points," chimed in Julia.

"It was fifteen, maybe twenty minutes. Okay it was like three or four Odeza tracks. No, maybe it was Aoki or that guy that Taylor Swift dated. Anyways, we went looking for her when she didn't come right back like she said she would."

Harper was sure it wasn't too long at all. "When we tried to go through the kitchen to get out to the back parking lot, these two huge bouncers blocked our way. We told them we didn't want any food, just our friend but they didn't budge."

"One was actually really good looking — 'member Harper? The one with the bag of Doritos?" added Julia.

"Buff as shit. The big dark haired Hawaiian guy was ring leader; kept telling his chain gang not to let us in the kitchen. They literally locked arms like a human chain so we couldn't get in. We figured that's where they had taken Jessie. None of us realized what was going on out back til it was too late."

They droned on about this or that bag of chips until finally *eureka,* they decided to go out and around.

It was dark and their stories varied on who went first, who saw what, nothing useful.

"Blood everywhere. Smelled like fire and mold. Hard to walk. Heels stuck in something or other."

Trying to get to their friend while walking on all that soft trash was like walking in quicksand. "People everywhere were fucking, or grinding. Some were puking. No one was helping her."

What they described from then on was tough to hear. They were sure she was dead.

"Her arm. Like I woulda helped her but there was so much blood. She wasn't moving."

"Oh my God' I was sure she was DEAD," cried Harper. "I couldn't even dial 911 my fingers would not work."

"Well I was gonna try to check for her pulse but...it was dark and it stunk so bad out there."

"We don't know who called the ambulance," Julia said somberly.

Jones couldn't take much more. Blotto kept waiting for one of them to give her the name Dewey or describe his freckle face, nearly balding fat head, but nothing doing.

She knew better than to lead a witness, but she simply had to ask, "Was there a big, fat red-headed guy with his belly hanging over his gym shorts?"

"Nope. Only athletic builds. Real big guys," chanted Julia; seemingly starry-eyed over that Doritos eater.

She reviewed her notes: two huge black guys; one Hispanic, not as huge, the two biggest guys looked like bouncers from the City. Mister Tall Dark and Doritos in the doorway to the kitchen.

At least eight in there; only saw one female who was 'allowed' in kitchen making out with a little guy. Out back too dark to describe any perps. Walking was difficult and 'like mushy.' Noted.

We need to go back out there. There has to be evidence somewhere. She had heard rumor of mattress parties indoors but maybe these ass hats lined their entire parking lot. "Ladies, can you remember anything else about the night. What you drank, who you danced with? Any names?"
Dealing with a batch of dimwits here.

"Like I said, that one girl. She looked like a rag doll the way they carried her up."

"Carried her where? Blond or brunette?"

"Brown hair."

"K, brown hair. Is that the victim or the hauler?"

"Both. Oh my God, I am not sure," tears again.

Troubling was the fact that again and again these ladies described a victim worse off than their pal. Where and who was she? What could be worse than a dislocated fracture on an unconscious naked female transported?

Wait. Maybe we call EDS or Alta Bates and find out if any transport personnel can ID any perps. "Okay ladies. We appreciate your taking a moment to talk with us. Here's my card. Please do not hesitate to call my cell there on the back if you can remember anything. I mean it, any detail at all about the party or the guys or your friend and what she maybe took last night."

PART III

SATURDAY

Headline: Alumni Weekend brings in record numbers

A record number of individuals and groups will descend upon the University campus today for tailgates, festivities, and a little 'sumpin sumpin' according to AD. 'Alumni arrive and enjoy reliving their glory days,' says Willard.

@GHB: LOL flipside. Babygotback. #longlivethebarge

@LEAD: If you are wondering 'what counts as sexual assault or harassment?' this is the thread for you #EROC@UCB

@ROOF: Buck the Ducks; RITNB; for you tards translation: RED IS THE NEW BLACK #gonnacryrape #jewsues #notmysister

@JD17: Barging Out; police shut down annual tailgate for the old guys. #gotparking #boatersfloatwithnowater

Frankie and Holly

When Frankie awoke about midnight on Holly's futon, she grimaced in pain.

"Have you got any Advil—uhm—what's your name again?"

111

Holly had been seated in the rocking chair nearly two hours by this time, trying to decide what to do. Recalling their earlier conversation. Holly's mother had suggested calling the police, but she really hated to rat someone out who had done nothing 'wrong,' so-to-speak.

"I really feel bad for her mom, and you know you'd do the same thing if you were in my shoes. I get all my compassion from your side as you always say."

"Which is why she needs medical attention, darling. Now then, the police will determine if she is fine to go home or if she needs to see a doctor. There are some really odd strains of the flu going around this year. Did you get your flu shot honey?"

"Yes, mom. Went to Walgreens and 'got a shot to give a shot' the day you called me about it." Mom had not been very helpful. What is the *right thing* to do she'd asked herself over and over until this moment.

Advil. YES, Advil. "On it." she popped up to the medicine cabinet and was back in a flash. Frankie had gulped down the entire glass of water and held it out towards Holly for an obvious refill. *My God this girl was not properly parented...no please or thank you...must have had a terrible upbringing.*

"Here you go." Frankie had helped herself to *four* Advil— Holly had only ever taken two at one time—and proceeded to down the second glass of water.

"So. Where the fuck am I and who the fuck *are* you?" shot Frankie.

"Well hello there, nice to meet you too," replied Holly. She spent about ten minutes going over the scene in the street, the Asian guy who had helped her get Frankie home, lg her up to her bedroom.

"I have no idea who opened the door to your place, but they were certainly very rude about it. Are your roommates not your friends?" she'd asked lly. "Not one person offered to help me help you up the stairs?"

As Holly detailed for Frankie the series of events, her brain drifted off momentarily. *Did Beau and I do it? Are we now officially an item? Should I talk to him about not seeing others...nah, too soon.* She was unable to determine if she was giddy from excitement or nauseous from the alcohol last night. She just didn't feel right but could not put her finger on it. *And the pain, coming in ebbs and flows, the bleeding...*

Holly and Frankie agreed there were parts of the evening needing clarification and that with her having missed practice last night, she needed to immediately check in with A and B, or Jane as soon as possible.

"Swear to me you won't tell a soul," snarled Frankie.

"I swear." Holly had become increasingly worried about what exactly had happened to this girl. Could she become pregnant from her encounter? Was there a drug now in her system that would get her in trouble with her team? Thankful for having

113

never had an athletic bone in her body, nor need to work out her size four frame, she ached with concern for this lost soul. "Just promise me you'll see a doctor about that bleeding we talked about." *Bleeding from your rear end really must mean something bad. Holly visibly shuddered at what this girl might have been through.*

"Not one word to anyone. Fuck, we've never even met." Frankie eased down the stairs of Holly's garage top apartment feeling each and every step as if she'd just finished a marathon run.

A new sadness came over Holly. She thought she'd made a friend last night.

Frankie made it back to her place fine, but the trip had taken all the drive she could muster. *I gotta just lay down for a bit, then I'll call—where's my cell phone? Shit. Did I leave it at that freak's apartment? Shit. Fuck. Damn. Sometimes I am SUCH an idiot. What if I really was? I need to. Man it hurts so dang, everything hurts. Why? I cannot stand it, I just wanna.*
Please no, tell me it didn't happen.

Officers

Jones and Blotto stopped at Starbucks on Oxford before heading back to the station. They took seats up top overlooking the famous gate to campus—there must be witnesses they had decided.

"With an entire house full of partiers, someone at some point witnessed something. We need to get back to the house and interview a few others," Blotto said matter-of factly.

"Do I need to remind you the Chief is not on board with all this?" argued Jones.

"No offense, but he's never been victim of a sexual assault..." she let that hang in the air for only a moment before adding, "that Stanford swimmer would have walked scott-free if it weren't for the two Swedes that came forward. All we need is one witness, one pair of sober eyes in or around that house last night."

Jones was still contemplating what she'd said. *Had Blotto suffered an assault way back and become a cop because of it? That'd explain her overzealous obsession with this case.*

"Who called the cops? Someone with half a brain dialed 911 for this Stanford girl, but everyone we spoke to is describing a victim inside the house 'getting it worse.' This shit has got to stop, Jones, and if I have to take it on myself, I will," her voice escalating.

"Look. All I said was Chief ain't on board—I am with you one hundred percent." Compassion filled his voice now.

He'd always felt protective of his partner, and with this tidbit of new information, he felt a pang of guilt for not catching on to it all before now.

She was a veteran on the force, but still requested weekend evening and night shifts. Three former partners had moved on and been promoted to day shift or detective; buzz about the station was Blotto had declined several department offers of advancement.

Munoz and Flint stood on the pavement for a few minutes before either spoke. Flint was only a freshman, he'd been raised by a single mom who'd repeatedly told him to do the right thing, 'see something say something,' never ever put yourself in a position to find trouble with the law.

"One of us has to go back in there," he said.

"Fuck no." Edgar was firm. "Deny until you die."

The two began the walk towards Shattuck, they'd catch a bus. Andre stopped at Milvia Street and couldn't take another step in good conscience.

"Look man, all we gotta say is they need to find that girl called Frankie. We don't know her, we never touched her, but she prolly needs to see a doctor or some shit." Andre had no idea...

"Fuck you." Munoz crossed and turned up Center Street, leaving Flint on the corner. He turned back just long enough to see that Flint was headed back to the station. *Mother fucker. Shit's gonna get real. I gotta check with my boys and get this shit straight like right now. Stupid fuckin drunk bitches can't hold their liquor now I gotta see the heat.*

She fuckin begged me to take her up...fuckin drunk bitches... John passed her up to Dewey on three was last I heard. Asshole better be home. Mother fucker.

Back to the station

Andre Flint gave a detailed statement to Chief Orzo being that detectives Monroe and Tazey were at the medical center, officers Jones and Blotto not back from the scene yet. Detailed in so far as drugs, sex, and techno music were rampant. He knew no one by name being he wasn't a boater. He, in fact, was *living* at the barge unexpectedly, and kept mostly to himself aside from the party.

Track and field was a seven days per week commitment. Andre was dedicated as hell to proving his worth to the team and his proud momma. His being caught up at the Barge was simply an unfortunate series of events beginning with there being no assigned dorm room the day he'd arrived on campus.

After taking the train up from Bakersfield, he'd been met by an assistant coach and dropped in front of Clark Kerr with very little information other than 'this is where most athletes live freshman year' and 'the food sucks.' He'd spent nearly an entire day sitting in the admin office waiting for a room number; a key; anyone willing to keep an eye on his duffel while he jogged to the track to ask Coach.

He was staying just another week at the barge until a shared dorm slot opened up. There was some mix up with him not having a room when he'd arrived on campus three weeks earlier. Coach told him to *"figure it out"* because he was only a partial scholarship athlete and frankly coach "couldn't give a shit *where* the kid slept as long as he wasn't late to practice."

Friend of a friend had told him he could crash on the floor in his room because the boaters were not in season. He'd just finished his laundry on Wednesday and felt like a big shot helping out these fine ladies in their quest.

Andre took a remorseful moment of thought. *His mother had carefully packed his underwear in a Ziploc baggie separate from the one with socks. Tucked lovingly into a small duffle that fit into the larger having his clothes and such. Shoes in the end pockets; keep the dirty in the mesh bag until wash day and be sure to plan ahead so as to not run out of clean...down two pair was gonna upset that applecart.*

He explained how that night he'd helped a couple of reds with their scavenger hunt. Terrified that if the police were to get their hands on his Jockey's, he'd be caught in some sort of story.

Two blondes dressed in red had approached him close to eleven pm. He'd escorted them up a flight of stairs, past a boater doggy-style with a naked brunette in the hallway. She did not seem to be bothered, or making any noise at all come to think of it.

He went on about partying and sex on the second and third floors inside being entirely different than the back lot. Mostly girls were not allowed upstairs in the house unless 'invited.' He'd seen his share of racy movies, but never could he have imagined sex screams at all hours of daylight or dark—even on school nights.

Andre described gaggles of drunks and folks screwing in every corner of the property—inside and out—during 'boat nights' and themed party evenings. It was a complete mystery to him how anyone outside the place would set foot on the Barge; if you knew the history or heard the stories. It was the last place you'd ever *choose* to live in his opinion.

He described the mattress-covered lot out back. Traditions being what they were with the boaters; stories to curdle your milk. Gang bangs, willing females bouncing from pad to pad naked and *not* afraid; straight up horror flick meets Eyes Wide Shut. Dozens of guy and girls all seemingly popping in and out of the mania at will.

He didn't know much about the drugs, but the garbage pail filled with alcohol was continually 'restocked' during parties when someone arrived with a bottle. Didn't seem to him that it was liquor specific—beers dumped in, vodka, whiskey, wine. Sort of what they called back home a smorgasbord.

Sure he'd seen pills of all colors sizes and shapes passed and popped, but he could not help in identifying any of it.

"Momma barely let us have an aspirin in my house." he'd explained. "No drugs whatsoever." And no, these did not look like ibuprofen or aspirin in his opinion.

Rubbing his temples Orzo'd made the decision to send out CSI. *Just once can I get a weekend without the headache of ANOTHER*

119

campus rape? That was what campus police were for; agencies aligned and plenty of UC personnel assigned to underage drinking, sexual assault, Greek life, bullshit, bullshit, bullshit that this landed on his turf again.

Berkeley PD

Blotto stormed into the building ten steps ahead of Jones. "Chief, we need to talk. Later Jones." Technically their shift had ended, Jones would head home.

Arm raised in her direction, Orzo interrupted her, "It's done. CSI is out at the Barge. They found the mattresses, bloodied garments. Shit for days. It's done."

"Wait, what?" Blotto was fuming. "This is my case and you don't tell me before…"

"Do I answer to you, Renee?" his voice had softened and he'd used her first name.

Holy crap. Shit's hittin the fan. Jones is already gone home for some shut eye. I'll just pop back over there to see what CSI is looking at. Renee could feel her blood pressure rise with this new development.

Barge

The crime scene crew is on site by mid-day. The unlucky officer assigned to keep gawkers off the property tugged away on a cigarette. Weekends always included drunk students and breaking up fights. The predictability of the nuisances was a normal Saturday. Homicide rumors brought tensions to next level.

He could hear the whispers from the crowd.

'Was there really a dead girl out back on those filthy mattresses?'

'I heard there were ambulances and fire trucks last night; somebody died.'

'Was it a Stanford swimmer?'

'That's what they're sayin.'

Couple of agents out back were scraping mattresses and bagging bloodied panties, a sock or two, a Cal football winter toque...the odd used condom.

"Hey guys, who wears a toque on a hot fall day." CSI Agent 1 is pleased with his find.

"Christ. They all do these days. Day, night, church-going, or straight chillin'. Who can figure where these cats get their style guides?" answers nearby Agent 2. "Bag it."

"Let's get it done and get outta here." The officer watching from the porch cannot stand the smell one minute longer. He'd been on the job only a few months and quite frankly, *did not sign up for this shit. Campus police would be shuttin' down parties, keeping the bikini clad drinkers on the porches, basically gettin into Cal football games free* was what he'd heard.

Agent 1 is newly charged up. "Hey, lookie here. A Stanford ID card."

They've got a couple dozen bags and its way past their lunch hour. "That's a wrap." Agent 2 is taking charge. As they head out, Officer Blotto approaches in plain clothes.

"Agent Feinstein, hello. Officer Blotto, on the scene last night. What've you got there?"

"None of your God damned business Blotto. Go home." He'd heard about her reputation for over—staying her welcome on the crime scene and making detectives look bad.

"No really. Can I just get a name off that ID for my report?"

"What makes you think I got an ID on me?" Feinstein is walking faster.

"Judd, seriously. Just the name."

"Says Jessica. Jessica Marie Tucker, you happy? Now get outta here. This is our case and you're off duty. Stay the fuck back." *Not wanting to get nasty but this bitch is nothing but trouble for the Detective Bureau.*

"Did you get the phone number from dispatch on the 911 call?"

"What the fuck do I want that for?" *Dammit. There's our witness.* Feinstein texted HQ.

"Here's my card. When you get the number, call or text me. I will run down the witness and deliver them directly to you." Blotto knew Feinstein couldn't turn down a free pick up—and maybe she'd get a few minutes in before they questioned him or her.

Athletics

Willard had been in the conference room with attorneys for hours. They'd conferenced in the heads of the MCGC and IFC, both of whom were 'out of cell range at a retreat,' they'd said. *Together. How cozy.* He'd talked with campus police as well as Berkeley PD.

Shutting down the Barge was the obvious first step. Clean up and clearing athletics being the larger concern. Berkeley PD griped about some sort of city trash issue. *What the fuck did they expect an athletic director to do about the fucking trash in the streets?*

"Andrea, can you please explain to me why Moore is not back from lunch at one fucking thirty—and don't give me that 'it's a Friday bullshit'—I texted him three times. Get his ass in here."

"Sir. He said something about having had a Monkey brew on the lunch hour, sir…I think…"

"Are you for real right now?" Willard was shouting at Andrea knowing full well she was his best assistant director. He suspected she was covering for that fuck up Moore. He had to

123

tread lightly with her as she knew about 'all the skeletons in all of the closets' as they say.

Moore had gotten wind of the 'situation' before 8 am and tried calling in sick but Andrea was not going there with Willard right now. She'd had no idea where he was, but it certainly was not business related. *Was he even in Berkeley* she wondered? Figures he holds the assistant athletic director position while she serves as assistant -- *gender bullshit on the daily.*

He strode out of the conference room and back to reception. "Sheila, get assistant AD Moore in here pronto." Pissed at himself for allowing Moore to keep a scheduled lunch date with someone from human resources. *WTF was Moore talking to HR for anyways? And now he thinks he can have a fucking beer at lunch with HR? Fuck him.*

What they'd put together so far was two, possibly three, victims; Stanford swimmers, Cal boaters, runners, basketball and football players all having had *'representatives'* at the party. A real shitshow of a scene at the corner of Piedmont and Bancroft with yellow tape. CSI investigators from the City; a police rodeo circus ring of epic proportions. Someone mentioned a mattress on the lawn?

Coaches were headed over from Palo Alto to meet privately with a couple of coaches here. He'd taken only one break in six hours and that was to *accept* some bullshit resignation letter from Coach Carter. Fuck him. No way was he getting outta this shit with a fucking piece of paper on the 'day after.'

Willard stewed. *I shoulda fired him last season. Nothing but bullshit coming outta that fuckin team. Best recruits in the state they freaking come in second to Washington the past five times at Pac 12's—second ain't shit—runner up don't mean shit. They supposed to win it this year. Ain't no way his ass is leaving now. Only swim and dive championships since taking over the department. This is some bullshit. Fuckin football and basketball assholes too—wtf. Water polo, rugby. Fuck. We oughta make rugby D1.* He was full of great ideas no one was listening to.

Willard was having what looked like an asthma or panic attack as Andrea rounded the corner. Last thing she wanted to say right now but here goes...

"Sir. I don't think we'll be seeing Martin today. I think we go ahead with his back up when meeting with the coaches. It's 1:45 and they are due in here by 2. There simply is no time to catch him up on it all."

"Andrea. While I appreciate your input, his ass better be seated in here by two or he's fired." Both Willard and Andrea knew this was just letting out steam, not exercisable—Moore knew too much.

"Yessir." She was off to set up the white boards they'd worked on earlier.

Jane

Early Saturday, Jane was deciding between a new cell phone and heading to Frankie's apartment, but wait, today is the big game and the frat on Haste was foaming up their entire lawn for a foam party. It was too big to miss.

"James. You are gonna love it, it's a foam party. Grab your swim trunks."

"Trunks huh?" he laughed and slapped her on the bare ass. "I got trunks."

They stopped at Noah's on the way for a bagel. *'To soak up the alcohol.'* Jane was so clever sometimes. James at twentysix had seen his fair share of big drinkers but this gal was top dame. He could hardly keep up this early, but she was swiping her credit card and ordering for both of them before he could say a word. *'Along for the ride.'* He laughed to himself.

"Member, I gotta be at work by eleven," he reminded her. "No alcohol for me."

"Oh my gahd, you are so responsible." She tickled his chin. "Let's just pop up to my apartment so I can grab my bikini. We'll get you all foamed up—see if we can't
corrupt you just a little bit."

They arrived before nine at the party. A and B were already hammered and coated in the white stuff. "Jane. Get the fuck in here," squealed Anne. "And who's the hunk? I didn't know Taye Diggs was on campus today. Oooooh weeeee."

"Oh my gahd Jane, they're awl talking 'bout Fwankie? Have you seen—was she waped?" Beth was slippery drunk already slurring her words at nine am.

"DRINK," shouted Marla. "Shotgun time." She was getting the hang of this crew pretty quickly.

The foam came from all directions and became a bit of a slipping hazard. That was before a few of them vomited from ingesting too much orally. No worries, party on, slippage expected and entertaining for all.

James did less than ten minutes of observation before dipping out. He'd call her later. She was shot-gunning a beer with her pals. No doubt she'd be blitzed in no time being still pretty tipsy from the night earlier. *Damn she was fine.* He looked back as he left—her head tipped backward, blonde hair falling over the bare back, blue striped bikini bottoms. *Sure wish it wasn't a work day.* James thought better of calling in sick and headed to work.

Party Girls

"Look, she made it perfectly clear to us that she wanted to be left alone with Beau Thursday night. It's not like we fuckin' ditched *her*, or some shit."

A nice hot slice at Artichokes Pizza was just what they all needed after a couple hours at the foam flat. The newly fashioned four-some was seated on the sidewalk with slices too large for the plates.

"Whatever Anne. It was not *our job* either way. Fuckin' Frankie and her buddy system, this one's on *you,* Jane." Beth bit into her pepperoni—she had a bit of alcohol to soak up with this pizza outing.

Marla was feeling a bit uncomfortable. It was mostly the drinking vodka starting at 8am but something was nagging at the back of her mind. Thoughts of her fateful night at Davis were popping up strong and loud the past two days. *Dammit all to hell. I transferred so I'd never have to relive those thoughts ever again.* She had never once spent time with Frankie or any of these girls prior to this weekend and suddenly they were her besties?

"I gotta go," she announced, as she stood up from her slice. "Homework."

"Homework? That's some bullshit. It's fucking Saturday." A and B agreed wholeheartedly with Jane's statement.

Marla hit the button to cross Durant but didn't wait for the 'white man walking' signal. She hustled across and headed home. Throngs of Bears-wear clad people impeded the straight shot, but she kept her mind on the destination and was home in twelve minutes. Tears welled up as she unlocked the door, full throttle sobbing began as she slammed her bedroom door and fell on her pillow.

"You okay in there?" She had female roommates but this was a male voice. She was not about to answer.

Beau

When Beau awoke on Saturday morning he had a renewed sense of confidence in himself. *Fuck those cops. Fuck Coach Carter. Fuck you Frankie.* He pulled on his blue and gold striped coveralls and rolled the cuffs up. Grabbing a bagel on his way out the door, he was headed out for a bit of foam fun.

"Dude, what up?" the hand-slap-shake-pound from John greeted him as he arrived at the party.

"Hey man." Edgar was looking down hoping to avoid any confrontation about the police question and answer session from Thursday night.

"Either of you mother fuckers got a clean cup for Beau Man?" he was ready to party.

Holly

Holly woke Saturday morning with a horrible sense of dread. Something wasn't right about simply letting Frankie walk home alone this morning. The bloodied and matted hair, her sweats reeked of month-old vinegar or wine, the nasty back talk and disjointed sentences. Maybe she had been drugged by some bath salts.

She'd heard a story on 60 Minutes about how people became erratic and volatile after having been drugged at a party. *That is probably what happened to Frankie*, and Holly needed to talk to her and explain how this all happens. *As Seen on TV.*

She wadded up the pillow case and blanket she'd lent her on the futon last night and dropped them out on the front porch for some air—Sunday is laundry day.

As she strode past the tailgate parties towards the library, she felt a pang of desire.

Should I try harder to get in with the "IN" crowd? The laughter and bikini-clad girls reminded her she really could not pull off that whole Kardashian-esk theme. Get your work done, then find time for play.

That girl Frankie sure had played Thursday night and look what that got her. Her inner voice talked her back out of wanting that life. She had priorities, being popular wasn't one of them.

Game Day Parties

The foam party and tailgates were poppin'. Big game against Pac12 rival Oregon brought in droves of thrill seekers, young and old.

The legacy men who had planned to park on the lawn at the barge were none too pleased to be told by police they'd have to "find another spot." On a day like today?

"Fuck off you pigs!" Dewey's father was drunk already.

All the money in the world cannot buy you tailgate bays at Cal on game day without at least a year of advanced notice. No freaking way they'd find space for the traditional barge boys BBQ hitch and trailer.

Enough is enough of this generation fucking with their *fine reputation* the past few years. Damn kids were runners up at IRA and Pac12s—drunk & disorderly reports— heads will roll. Dewey's father and the other legacy men were cussing and fighting amongst themselves about who was to blame for this shit getting so outta hand.

Like father, like son, as the saying goes.

Tailgates begin set up around 6:30 am on big game days. Portable tents, toilets, tables and chairs all special ordered by this or that group. Campus police were on site beginning at 5am football Saturdays directing traffic, checking parking passes, and assuring smooth set up and exit of delivery trucks. The corner of Piedmont and Bancroft with yellow tape and police operations vehicles made one hell of a log jam. Looky-loos strained their necks to get a peek. Blocked off roadways and sidewalk in front of the Barge added fuel to the curiosity. A true logistical nightmare for campus police and staff.

Hatchbacks and pop-up picnics all across campus were abuzz about the police tape, the boaters BBQ being upended on an important alumni date. There were rumors of potential police involvement in a rape or gang bang or underage drinking or noise

131

violations or football players who might be suspended from today's game for any of the aforementioned accusations.

"How fuckin stupid can you be to fuck up on alumni weekend?" passersby wondered aloud of the boaters. "Look at these old guys with nowhere to party." Some of them laughed.

"Damn straight the football players ain't throwin' no fuckin party until *after* the game ya dipshits." So many walking by offering up 20/20 hindsight information on this fine football morning.

A representative from the women's boating team was trying to work out a way to share their lawn with at least the BBQ trailer in exchange for free eats. No one seemed to be in charge at the barge from inside, police still on scene and all, she was taking the bull by the horns if you will.

"Sir. If you can just get that trailer turned around at University and Piedmont, then come back towards Haste," the nice young lady offered. The streets were practically parking lots starting at seven am on days like today. Dewey Sr. was not in the mood.

"BRYCE," he yelled out again and again. No one from inside the house had come to the door just yet. He banged again. This time hollering to police about breaking the damn door down.

"Sir. We are only going to ask you one more time. Please stay off the porch—stay clear of this property altogether, this is a crime scene. There may, in fact, be no one inside for all we know."

Patrol officers from campus police were uncertain as to who was in charge and what was going on. Thankfully Berkeley PD were on scene.

Back at the women's house of boaters, there is scuttlebutt about a curler accusing their star male athlete of rape. It's just a few of them awake for now in the kitchen making finger sandwiches for the alumni tea midmorning.

"Was it that brunette I always see skanking around?" female boater 1 asks.

"How dare she cry rape when she clearly came on to him numerous times from what I heard," female boater 2.

"Betches, curling ain't even a real sport for fuck's sake. How dare she come on to Bow then accuse him of a damn assault, such bullshit."

"I agree. She throws herself at a different sport every season. Last year she was doin' half the football team. What does he even see in her? Hmph."

"Are you fucking kidding me? Beau is *dating* her?" Female boater 3, " I seen her ass all tight tailed and drunk off her fuckin' ass many times. Bullshit she tryna call rape now."

"Uhm. Is she the one at Berkeley Medical Center though? That's some gnarly shit if so." Another gal has entered the kitchen on the tail end of the chatter.

Silence fills the room as eyes swing this way and that.

Jane and Police

On Jane's front porch are two chairs and a hammock for chilling out. This is no chill scene.

"What the fuck are you talking about?" "Hey. So. Is Frankie ok?" Jane is alone on the porch of her apartment Saturday afternoon with two campus police detectives. *How odd that they seemed to appear in the five minutes she'd popped home to change clothes.*

"Can you tell us, please, who is Frankie? Her full name please, and how you two might be acquainted?" Officer 1.

"Well. Yes. Frankie is. Was. My best friend." *I'm still so damn pissed she hasn't called.* With that thought she realized her mind might be a bit pickled after three straight party days and nights. "*Is* my best friend. She's *ALIVE,* isn't she?" suddenly overwhelmed the flood gates open. *OMG. Frankie is dead. Dead and I was all freaked out that she hadn't call me?*

"Ma'am. We are here to ask you for information that might help us identify this friend of yours, Frankie. And to get a statement about your potential involvement at a party Thursday evening at the Boat House." Officer 2. "Identify? Wait. What? Identify her body?" the officers exchange rolled eyes.

"Sorry." It's a full four minutes before Jane can catch her breath from the hysteria to even speak. "I am soooo sorry." *Fucking boaters. Why did we even go there? We coulda just played some Cards Against Humanity with the freshmen and then danced on the rooftop to Drake. Damn frat parties. OMG. Frankie's dead. DEAD?* "Can I see...see her?"

"Miss. No one is dead, that we know of." Officer 1 is losing patience. *How can these coeds be freaking drunk by mid-day every day and still function? Obviously this one was not functioning. What a drip. Academic excellence at Cal, humph!*

"Oh my God. She's alive? Can I see her?" Jane is wide-eyed.

"How about we start with her *name,* kiddo?" Officer 2 is equally annoyed.

"Frankie. Well. I think it's really Francesca. No, wait. Francis. Yes, her name is Francis." elated and animated with her accomplishment.

"Okay then. Can you give us a *last* name?" Officer2. *This is gonna take all fucking day.*

"Yeah, well, no...wait...let me think." It's been two years but they never actually signed a lease together. What the heck is her— "Try Smith. I think it's Smith but spelled sorta European like with a Y."

"Smith?" Officer 1. *Are you fuckin kiddin me right now? Oakland. I gotta get reassigned to Oakland where the freaks are truly worth investigating—this bullshit college drinking drivel is gettin' old.*

"How about we take you downtown to help you remember a bit clearer?" Officer 2 is ready for a lunch break.

Barge Alumn

Blake Laskey has seen about enough. He is parked roadside in front of the Barge, watching what looks like an episode of CSI Campus. Some dippy broad is trying to convince Dewey to BBQ a block or two over, but it's time to get to the bottom of this story.

"Okay, Officer. I can see that you have been assigned to keep the peace, but you certainly have a price." Flipping through a quick stack of Franklins, he pulls $500 and reaches out.

"Sir. With all due respect. You need to put that money away and get the hell out of the street before you're ticketed or towed. I am not messing around." Officer Dussledork has seen these cats before. Pushing dollar bills around thinking they're above the law. *Oughta fucking write him the ticket right here, right now.*

"My son lives—"

"Dude. If your son is in this building right now, he oughta get the hell out and fast. This ain't no joke. This here's a crime scene."

"Crime? Honestly. Drunk students is hardly a crime. We have this lawn every game."

Dusseldork is losing his patience. Cars are backed up three blocks honking and barking. He reaches his back pocket for the ticket book.

"Okay. Okay. Now, wait a minute. I am moving, but really take this...for your trouble." he extends a single hundred dollar bill.

"No trouble you can buy your way outta today, sir. This place is shut down. Now get back in your vehicle and move out—you're causing a backup."

"How do you mean shut down? It's alumni weekend and we *already paid* for two days on the lawn."

Officer D is done with Laskey. He steps behind the vehicle to get the plate.

"No. Seriously man. You can't ticket me. I pre-paid."

"Blake. Whadda ya gettin outta this guy?" Dewey Sr. is also double-parked and with half the block in length towing the rolling grill.

"Bullshit. A whole bunch of BS about a crime and our spots being tied up. They can't do this. We all fuckin prepaid the entire lot."

"Lemme talk to him." All 325 pounds of Dewey Sr. taking strides towards Dusseldork.

Out of the corner of his eye Dusseldork sees a large figure approaching and draws his tazer. Officer D has already been called a pig by this one, *not on my watch mister*. In a blink, Dewey Sr. is down.

137

"What the fuck." Laskey drops to his knees next to Dewey Sr.

Three additional officers are on the scene almost instantly, hand-cuffing both Laskey and Dewey Sr.

Back at hospital

Jessica had very little to offer investigators. She had no recollection of being alone with any male offender. Did not want to press charges, and was refusing a rape kit.

"Honey. Please. You must remember something about the other night," her mother was back in the room and still crying.

"Mom. If you love me, get me out of here. Dad is blowing this all out of proportion and I just want to go home—to my apartment. Harper has her car. I will call you on Sunday like normal."

"Yes. Mrs. Tucker. I can get Jess back to campus."

"Absolutely not. You have a displaced fracture on that arm and you will not be able to even dress yourself. You are coming home with us and that's final." Dad had returned. No use arguing with him.

"As for your assailant. You do not need to be paraded in front of the news media over some incident that may or may not have occurred. I have instructed my attorney to take the matter up with the University in covering your medical expenses. This is not on you honey. Those frat boys, and the University of California, are going to *pay*."

"Thanks Dad." Jessica was at that instant so thankful for her 'helicopter father' and his 'controlling' self. So many times she'd hated him for meddling in her life. This time, she simply closed her eyes and thanked the universe for *anyone* willing to get her the hell out of this hospital room.

The only part she cared about was Dad will take care of it. She didn't have to talk to any more cops or doctors, Dad hired a lawyer, she'd not have to say another word. She closed her eyes to pretend to sleep, or so she thought. Out cold. The nurse checked blood pressure and heart rate.

"Roberta. If you would kindly assist my daughter in getting dressed. We will take her back to Monterey with us and follow up with our own Orthopedic surgeon on how to move forward in repairing that arm."

It was becoming apparent to everyone in the room that Mr. Tucker was not negotiating, and he'd be getting Jessica up and out of this place as quickly as possible. He was completely oblivious to the fact that she had again lost consciousness.

Roberta on the other hand was having none of it.

"Sir. With all due respect, we have not yet acquired even a urine test to be certain that your adult daughter is not in fact pregnant. If you will allow me to check her vitals, I believe she is slipping into a deep sleep anyways."

Silence. Eyes back and forth around the room.

"Frankly. I would like to ask that you and your wife return to your home and wait for a call from your daughter, if and when the time is right. For today, she is not going anywhere until the swelling in the arm will allow for proper stabilization." She quietly pushed the call button for back up.

"I can stay," Harper chimed in.

"Yes. We'll get a rolling chair bed in for her friend to stay the night. But I think its best you two meet with your attorneys elsewhere." She slipped an oxygen mask over Jessica's face.

Roberta had been annoyed earlier when Mr. Tucker insisted she provide him use of an office suite with fax machine and such so that he could properly sue involved parties. He seemed completely oblivious to the fact that a rape had occurred and Jessica would most likely need a psychiatric evaluation and/or counsel before being let go. Standard protocol when law enforcement brings in a patient in her condition.

"Sir. I want to remind you that when your daughter arrived at our facility for care she was unresponsive. We have tests and protocol that must be followed before we can simply release her—especially having the extent of injuries she has obviously incurred." To say nothing of the fact that she seemed completely out of it. She kept that to herself for now.

"Mrs. Tucker. With all due respect, your daughter is still in shock and must be properly treated for the extensive injuries suffered internally and externally. She will not be released before Sunday morning in my opinion. Quite frankly, you look like you could use a good night's sleep and a regroup. Your husband has so steadfastly assembled his legal team and plan—which will need to be orchestrated on a site other than this wing at the medical center. We will call you should there be any medical concerns at all that Jessica would like for you to be made aware of."

"Jessica *cannot take care of herself*, just look at her," she wailed.

Roberta took three strong strides towards Mr. Tucker. "This is not helping your daughter to recover from her incident, sir. It's time the two of you left." It was not a question or a gentle request, but an order.

The crash cart crew came barreling in.

For a second, Jess came to. She was flat on her back with the weight of an ocean on top of her. Faces came in and out of focus. Sounds were mostly of rowdy party goers, laughter. *Was that grunts and groans? Wait.* Someone was on her, or in her. There was a strange roar in her ears; pounding or thumping. She was sinking, or melting.
Sobbing and thrashing. She awoke in tears of hysteria.

"You're okay, dear. We are right here. You're okay."

Who? What? Jessica's brain was not working properly.

Her heart was pounding. There was a ringing noise in her ears. She could hear sobbing and felt trapped or caged.
Wait. It's me. I'm the one making those sounds. I'm sinking.

"I...can't...breathe," she gasped between weak breaths.

"Oh. You're breathing, Jessica. Now. Let's try to slow it down. How about an inhale on one and then a nice long inhale on two. One. In. Two. Out."

"Where am I? My head. Oh my gawd. Is this a hospital?"

Like a bad movie, the memory of her mother and father talking over her, and the ambulance ride. Then the party.

It all began to come back to her in a reverse fashion. The scavenger hunt. Uber to Berkeley. Pre-gaming at Angie's place. The D&G red dress she'd 'borrowed' from her mother's closet. Two words came out.

"The dress."

"Oh. I know these old gowns are not very stylish honey, but you look just fabulous after your big nap." Nurses could be so detached.

"The dress. I borro—I need to get mom's D&G to the cleaners." She was out again, but with better vitals this time.

"You're gonna be just fine." the nurse said to unconscious Jessica.

PART IV

SUNDAY

Headline *Daily Cal: Campus Sexual Assault a Daunting Epidemic*

Campus security issued an email alert warning of the uptick in sexual assaults on campus. The email provided contact information for the Counseling and Psychological Services at the Tang Center, UC Berkeley's health center, which provides medical and mental health services to students, and suggested that if you or a friend are concerned, to please seek medical or mental health care.

@JJ: getchu some, then deny you liked it #ladyinred

@Annon: don't blame the stud messengers; she asked for it. #longlivethebarge

@GHB: LOL peeps be hatin. Goin dark. #longlivethebarge

Player Development Center Berkeley

Coach Reid sat at his desk browsing 'affordable holiday vacation destinations,' when he heard someone click through the entry door to Stinson. It was an annoyance to say the least, having the first office from the door, but curling was hardly an income-generating sport so he'd remind himself regularly the fact that he even *has* an office is a luxury.

This athletic department was by far the wealthiest he knew of or had ever seen; he'd been in quite a few over the years. Sponsors seeking exposure in the states went all out to secure the top universities—Nike providing all the footwear and clothing imaginable to all sports just to have Football and Basketball. As head coach, he had the difficult task of choosing each season; shoes for ice, travel, and practice. Shorts for workouts, long pants for matches, travel and play, long sleeve, short sleeve, no sleeve—it all really was a hoot. He'd sent a toque back home to his father-in-law last year and was still reaping the rewards for having made the gesture.

When the team got a locker room and two coaches offices a couple years back he was not about to complain about locale. One for him and privacy, the other for grad assistants and trainer. State of the art facility, weight room stocked with enough power drink and bars to feed a country, ice baths, rehabilitation room, laundry—it really was the *Ritz of Rec*. Only a handful of universities even offered the sport, much less offices with doors to close out the riff-raff and key cards.

He could access the log at any time to see which, if any, of his squad was utilizing the facility weight room or study center. Never ever did he bother as he fully understood the futility of that. It wasn't even seven am on a Sunday morning, far too early for even the most ambitious football player to be swiping in for ice baths.

He looked up just in time to see Frankie appear in his door window; a battered and bruised face resembling her anyways. *What the hell?* He jumped up to get the door and flung it open as she fell into an unrecognizable jumble of tears and apology on his futon couch.

From what he could gather, she surely had good reason to have missed practice yesterday. Apart from that, he had not gotten anything comprehensible out of her for nearly ten minutes when his grad assistant Landry popped in. *Phew. This is a prime time grad assistant moment.*

"Let me go for Starbucks while you two catch up," he offered softly. He pulled his chair back and gave a Vanna White wave towards it for Lan. "Text me your orders ok, Lan. I'll be right back." And he was out the door.

Quit freaking calling me Lan. Landry allowed it only among her friends—certainly not Coach Reid, fuckin poser. *Of course, he's gonna get coffee. WTF.*

Frankie had sobbed and sniveled for nearly an hour before Coach returned. Lan was beside herself trying to calm and reassure this bag o' bones, cussing under her breath at Reid for leaving her like this.

Lan was no MSW, no Nurse Nancy. She had not signed on to hear these prissy bitches go on about some ass wipe athlete sexual encounter gone wrong. She was only in this morning to use the elliptical without interruption.

She'd done her four years on the squad and heard plenty of these 'he used me' stories. Granted this one came with quite a colorful set of bruises and a black eye—God damned boater barge. When were these ladies gonna learn? Boys being boys is one thing; bastards being bullies was expected at the barge.

"Here we are," in his best cheer 'em up voice. "How are you two making out…I mean…coming…I, well…how's things?"

Reid was careful around Lan knowing full well she was not out to the team yet.

His awkward splatter was annoying. "Oh, we good," replied Landry. "Real good. Like yeah. We both woke up early thinking let's get our workout in," she added sarcastically. "I think you'd better call Karen." With that, Landry swung her towel around her neck and headed for the equipment room.

Karen was the athletic trainer assigned to curling and a few other women's sports at Cal. She was truly a mother hen and Coach was kicking himself for not thinking of it first. As he dialed her cell, he realized it was not a match day and he might be waking her. She answered on the first ring.

"Karen here." She sounded a bit out of breath and was talking into her iWatch.

"Listen, sorry to bother you," he began not taking notice of the faint distance of her voice or wind rasping into the earpiece.

"Ah. No bother but I am in the middle of a half marathon in the City, Coach. It's an emergency?" heavy breathing.

"Uhm well. Yes...I mean no...well yes. We do need Frankie to *see* someone." Coach was not at all interested in explaining the look of this kid *or* what he suspected to have happened to her.

"Yup. Well get her to Tang walk-in buddy. I'm out." She'd hung up.

Karen was used to Coaches calling at all hours expecting her to simply drop everything for their calls. *Medical attention was an easy one you idiot. Dial 911 or head to urgent care. Jeez these coaches were simpletons.*

Coach and Frankie

As they drove to the Tang Center walk in clinic, not one word was spoken. Coach Reid knew this was not something he wanted to explore. Frankie seemed in some sort of trance.

"Chief complaint this morning?" chimed the triage nurse.

"Uh...well... Our trainer is doing a half—" Coach again fumbling for words.

"Miss. Can you tell me your name and why you are here this morning?" She interrupted him and redirected her inquiry.

Frankie began to cry. The nurse looked up at Coach. "I'll take it from here, sir. Are you her father? Maybe you'd like to step over to the desk there and provide her insurance information."

Coach Reid breathed out a sigh of relief—that lasted only a second before he panicked. *Should I need to call her parents?*

At that exact moment, his cell phone rang. It was a 415 number he didn't recognize and he let it go to voicemail.

Not today. Not. One. More. Thing.

He waited until the buzzing stopped and called Landry. She didn't answer so he left a message. "Lan. I gather I owe you one, but I need a favor."

Frankie

Frankie was grateful that coach left, while at the same time felt an odd longing for someone to hold her hand. Unsettling as hell being she prided herself on being selfsufficient, tough as nails; *leadership material* as her high school coach always liked to refer to her. A *confident core* her mother phrased it dozens of times. My *champion and hero,* her dad lovingly added most days.

This body she lay in—flat on her back with heels in stirrups—was anyone but that girl. There was no confidence, strength or heroism in what she was feeling emotionally, or physically, as the doctor poked and prodded up inside her.

Was this the result of too much to drink or did she have to begin to think about the painful realization that maybe—oh God please no—did she have sex with someone that night? If she couldn't remember it, did it in fact happen?

For all the confusion, she still began convulsive tears over the invasion of her personal space then and now. A violation of her person at the very core. A soiled and rancid taste boiled in her mouth. She'd unknowingly bit into her bottom lip and now tasted the coppery flavor of her own blood. Surely she was going to be sick...

"Swab," the doctor demanded. "Just a pinch now. Another swab, please." *WTF was she shoving up her ass?*

Tears flushed down the sides of her face into her ears.

Pushing penetration thoughts away momentarily, she closed her eyes and tried to imagine being anywhere but on this cold parchment table. The sound of the crackling sheet was a welcome distraction from the words she continued hearing bellowed from doctor to nurse. Gripping the sides of the paper, staring up at the black holes in the ceiling tiles thinking maybe she could try counting them...ouch...close your eyes and count to ten.

"Fuck," she called out. She'd been trying with all her might to keep her mouth shut.

"Very sorry," his voice at least a bit more at ease. "Just one more."

One more what? Jeez this was way beyond the standard pinch and poke of her annual exam. *What is there to see down there?*

"Okay. One...more...stitch." *Wait. What?*

"Stitches. What the fuck?" she'd held her tongue for the last fucking hour of this bullshit, now she needed answers.

"Francis. You need to hold still just a bit longer." Nurses always use the sing-song tone.

"It's Frankie. I told you ten times. Frankie, not Francis. And I think it's my right to know what the fuck is going on with *stitches* going into *my* body?" There was her tough self at least in her voice—she wiped tears away and attempted to sit up. No strength. A feeling of weightlessness and helplessness the tears started up again.

"Not yet dear. You are under sedation and won't be feeling a thing."

"Drugs? You gave me drugs without telling me?"

"No dear. Not drugs. Just a local anesthetic so the doctor can do a little light repair down there. You've had quite a shock this weekend and—"

Oh my God. Her voice is fucking killing me.

"I freakin' came in here just to get a damn after the fucking morning pill or some shit. Don't you freakin' call my parents before you start surgery or some shit like that?" She fell back on the plastic pillow sobbing. *WTF is happening here? Why did I let him bring me? How long is this gonna fucking take? I just want to go home. Home. Home. I have had it with fucking Cal and fucking Berkeley. Was fuckin Coach Reid still here?*

"Wait. You didn't call my parents, did you?" she blinks back to the stark cold of the room and the white ceiling, and the fact that she's on a medical table with rods and clamps stickin' out of her privates. Or is it her asshole? *Oh my God. Oh my God. What happened to me? What is going on?*

Head is pounding, hands are shaking. *Why are they lookin' up my ass? This is disgusting. Why is it I cannot remember Thursday's party? We pre-gamed as usual. Beau...wait. Beau left me to get a drink. What. Who...I danced...it was Aoki...who is the girl I keep seeing in my mind? How is it Sunday already?*
Seriously. Did I have sex on Thursday???

Suddenly she was shivering cold. *Breathe.* Think.

Tears begin to flow again while gripping the bed sides. Her best attempts to *wish it all away by visualizing a beach and blue water somewhere far, far away* trick was just not working.

"Okay then. All set." *Fucking doctor is so fucking proud of himself with that white coat and shit-eatin' grin on his face. Fuck you.*

As if hypnotized to do so, Frankie fell into a deep sleep with a snap.

Frankie

Frankie was groggy as she woke to white walls and a strange beeping noise. Turns out she'd lost enough blood during the stitches and such the nurse put her on a monitor when she'd passed out cold. How long had she been here / asleep? What the heck was that beeping noise?

The bruising of her arm was immediately alarming to her mainly because she'd seen what her face looked like in the mirror on Saturday but there had been nothing wrong with her arm.

"Good afternoon, dear. Don't worry about that bandage and bruising, we had to draw some blood and your veins were not cooperating." a sing-song voice again.

She then remembered the doctor and talk of stitches and the intake clerk at Tang giving her quite an odd look. "And we started a line of fluids just as a precaution when you went into such a deep sleep."

"Can I have some water, please?"

"Yes, of course, dear. I'll be right back." As the nurse exited the room a wave of tears erupted. *What have I done and why all the equipment attached? I really, really, really want to go home. But oh man, thank gawd I am not at home for this little bit of action. I need to talk to Jane. How long have I been asleep? My head is aching, my hands are shaky and my legs are not cooperating. I cannot get up. Jane.*

As if summoned by angels, Jane appeared in the doorway.

"Can I come in?" Frankie had never heard Jane timidly ask anything. *Holy crap. Wait. She shouldn't see me like this.*

"Oh gawd, Frankie." Jane threw herself onto the bed and knocked over the metal stand attached to rubber hosing. "I thought you were *dead*."

"Ouch. Oh shit. Get the nurse. There's blood." Frankie's IV had come unplugged in the commotion of Jane's bear hug.

"Blood? I can't." Jane was quickly up and backed against the wall as the nurse returned with a styrofoam cup and straw.

"Oh dear. Well I suppose it was going to come out somehow." She seemed indifferent by the sight of the blood. The dangling cord spilling fluid all over the floor. It was Jane's white sheet of a facial expression that commanded her attention.

"Let's get you a chair, honey." the nurse casually acknowledging that Jane might faint based on the color of her face. *That's more important than me bleeding out?*

"Oh. Just put a little pressure on that spot Francis and I'll grab the gauze wrap." Back out the door went the nurse. *Geez a person could bleed to death on her watch. Fucking Francis. Who names a girl Fucking Francis?*

Neither Jane nor Frankie spoke. *Oh my God she looks horrible.* They thought to themselves about the other.

Marla

Sunday evenings were reserved for quiet reflection, and well, gossip along with red wine; rehashing the excitement of the weekend on college campuses. A and B had invited Marla to join them for homemade dinner—pasta boiled and red sauce poured over—she felt compelled to go.

"What can I bring?"

"Just your smiling face. Oh, and a bottle of red." *How in the world was she going to buy alcohol?*

As she scooted away from Trader Joes with a bottle of cranberry bubbly—nonalcoholic—she planned to act surprised if anyone called it out. *Honestly, these girls are so dumb they may not notice.* She smiled to herself.

Marla was surprised and thankful that Jane wasn't around when she'd arrived. She didn't dare ask if she'd be joining. It was just incredibly uncomfortable when the foursome gathered; she in the "Frankie" position. As enamored with them as she'd been from afar, getting to know this clique was quickly tarnishing the veneer. They literally dressed alike, spoke alike, walked together and had begun to look alike too. *No way am I cutting the neck and sleeves off my hoodie—eeew.*

"So, do you think you'll replace Frankie at Regionals?" Beth ever so direct.

"Gosh, I doubt it. I really—"Marla was thankfully interrupted, as this was not a topic she was interested in pursuing.

"I guarantee it, Beth. Frankie just skipped practice and didn't even text coach."

"What we really want to know is did you get anywhere with that cute rugby boy you were talking to yesterday?

Did he catch up to you? We saw him chase after you like a love sick puppy when you left so fast."

Beth was a touch annoyed being she had invested a few moments on the guy couple of weeks back. He'd snubbed her and she'd determined him to be "a closeted gay".

"I really had a lot of work to do yesterday." *Hmmm. Maybe it was Sven Riggons at the door—thank the lord I didn't answer with red swollen cry baby eyes.*

"Beth. Get over it. He was just not that into you. Doesn't mean Marla can't shag him."

As they ate and went on about boys and booze, Marla couldn't help but wonder about the obvious MIA Jane and Frankie.

"Is Jane out with James tonight?"

"Holy shit. How'd you catch his name? I swear I asked her four times and she never answered me—bet she thought I'd try to blow him—bitch has never forgotten freshman year."

"You know what Anne, I would not let any guy I liked within twenty fuckin feet of you, and your mad-dog tongue action. She's legendary. The guys love it. Swear they beg her. One guy tried offering her money; fuckin hilarious." Beth was really cracking herself up.

"Fuck you." A.

"Fuck you harder." B.

Back at Tang Medical Center

Jane stayed just long enough to hear that Frankie was getting cleaned up to check out when she realized she had forgotten to text James. Sunday was his day off, she needed an out and fast.

"Listen. It's my friend James' day off so we're gonna grab a Brazil boat—you want me to drop one off to your place later?" Offering food but no escort outta here was the best she could muster.

"Nah. Not hungry. So, who's James?" *Fuck you too, Frankie.* Jane was supposedly her 'best friend' and now couldn't even look her in the eye.

"If you change your mind, text me." Jane was already out the door not really listening for her reply.

"Golly. Your friend certainly was in a hurry. Is there someone I can call to come get you?" Charge nurse on the floor, Stacey, entered somberly. She seemed kind enough, but tears began to flow again.

"Listen. We need to talk before you get released Francis, I mean Frankie." *A for effort. Talk about what?* thought Frankie.

"Now, you don't need to say a thing, but I want to read from this pamphlet I am going to send home with you." *Great fuckin reading rainbow, here we go.*

"You came to us in pretty bad shape this morning, and according to your coach you told someone you had been feeling drugged or 'not yourself' since late Thursday evening. It is standard procedure when we see a young female patient who is showing signs of confusion or lethargy to test their blood sample for unusual or illegal drugs, so that we know what we are working with." She looked directly into Frankie's eyes with an 'are you following me?' *look.* "I am not saying that you are a drug user per se, but your sample did come back positive for GHB and Rohypnol."

"Per say? Rohipwhat?" *Jesus Christ was this turning into a drug bust by coach?* "What the fuck?" Anger slowed the tear flow.

"Franci...Frankie...I want you to slow your breathing. Think back to Thursday night. I am not accusing you. I am asking you to think back to the last time you had clear thoughts—help me to determine if you might have been ruffied—with a date rape drug."

"Date rape. Wait. What?" *Shit. It really was way back to think about Thursday and getting ready for the party.* She'd been so hype to seal the deal with Beau, but honestly she could not place he and she together like that. *For fuck's sake. Did I sleep with Dewey?*

"I really don't think I had sex with anyone in the past three weeks." *That was God's honest truth.* She'd been working on Beau for nearly a month and between practices, getting her apartment set up—there had been no one—not even a Tinder date in at least a month.

"Well. Let me be as frank with you as I would hope someone to be with me. You did in fact have sexual intercourse, and anal penetration, in the past couple days. If you'd like for me to have the doctor come back in to go over your stitches and such again."

"Wait. What doctor?" The memories were jumbled and beginning to feel out of body-ish. *Anal penetration? WTF? Fuck. Fuck. Fuck.*

"Okay. Now this is exactly what I mean. You had two conversations with Dr. Singh; one prior to the vaginal exam, swabs, repair of your torn rectum, and one afterwards. If in fact the drugs are still in your system, you may not recall details from those conversations and I can ask him to come back."

"Oh God, no please. Just tell me. What the fuck happened and why am I feeling so out of it?" Frankie felt like she'd lived a month in the past seventy two hours. Vague recollections of dancing with whom? Waking up in Dewey's room. Some girl appearing over and over again in her dreams. *Wait. That wasn't a dream.* I stayed at some rando's apartment Friday night. And she'd slept the entire day Saturday barely getting up to eat or pee—hell when was the last time she'd showered? *Is it still Sunday?*

"Ok. With your permission, I would like to invite a friend of mine in to talk to you. It's a friend from my old neighborhood as a kid. I'd trust her with my life, and she's been waiting for over an hour to speak with you."

"What are you talking about? A friend of yours wants to meet me? This is all fuckin nuts." *Sheesh. When is my brain gonna turn back on for reals?*

"Look. I don't want to freak you out any more than you already seem to be but my best friend growing up is a local cop. She went to the academy, I went to nursing school—usually *'I call her when I need help,'* but today she came in asking me to speak to you." Stacey paused. "Turns out you attended quite a party Thursday night—sounds like it resulted in a 911 call and an ambulance ride for another party-goer. Someone showing similar signs of not remembering much—her blood test came back eerily similar to yours and..."

"What the fuck are you saying..." *blood, ambulance. I just came in for a freaking morning after pill.*

"Hello, Frankie. You're a tough gal to track down. I have been looking for you for three days." Renee Blotto eased into the room and spoke slowly.

Is this bitch for real? Are we in remedial ed? Frankie was even more confused now.

"Don't be alarmed. I am on my day off. This is not me the police, it's me Renee, friend of Stacey's."

POLICE

Blotto went into the entire story. She gave Frankie a fair amount of background on the setting from Thursday but no clear memories were forming.

Frightened and freaked out, the story was just not adding up. *Why can't I focus? Think Frankie. Why was Jane acting so standoffish? I never saw any police. Nothing.* Lucid memories had been impossible to assemble for days now.

GHB was a liquid with no odor or color. Rohypnol is a pill that dissolves in liquid. *Shit that party pail punch?*

Some girl from Stanford landed in the hospital Thursday night with a broken arm and both drugs in her bloodstream. Assault, great bodily harm. A probable rape—not willing to prosecute. Won't talk.

I remember nothing after about 10:30pm Thursday. Friday and Saturday were nearly complete blurs. Do not start crying again. If I start again I may not stop. There it was again. Rape. Why can't I remember anything?

She described the party scene. The red dresses arriving. Some sort of squabble out back. Beau had given the police her name as early as Friday afternoon but they'd had trouble finding her until this morning. *Where the fuck was Beau? Shit. Did I text him this morning? Fuck. Coach. Where is he now? What does he know?*

"I wonder if you'd be willing to give me a statement in the next day or two when I actually am on duty." Frankie had only heard bits and pieces the past nine minutes or so. "It could even be 'off the record,' if you'd feel better that way."

"I uh...I have...uhm, honestly, I don't know what I can tell you. I don't remember a thing since early Thursday night." *Straight truth.*

"If you'd be willing to let me drive you home, I could leave you my card and you could think about it. Truth is, we cannot shut down these cowards drugging females at parties unless someone is willing to come forward with their drug results. We'd keep your name completely confidential."

"No. No way."

Fuck. She needed a ride home but confidential my ass— everyone was probably already talking about her for missing practice and then talking to Landry. Someone had already given her name to the cops. *Off the record, my ass.*

"I really don't think I can help you."

"Frankie." Stacey cut in. "I want to finish up with what I was reading to you earlier. Renee, do me a favor and pull your car around the front. I'll bring her out."

Just sitting up was causing Frankie an unusual amount of effort. She couldn't quite work out how all of these parts fit together.

"Listen. These things happen, okay? You did nothing wrong, and you're gonna be fine in a matter of days. But I can't let you go without telling you how I see this."

"Who even *are you* and why are you spending so much time reading me bedtime stories?" *Yea. That was rude. I don't give a fuck. I'm tired.* Frankie wanted out, and her own bed to cry in.

"I am an older and wiser, and currently medically trained version of you. I *was you* just a few short—well, about ten years ago, Frankie. Honest as shit, it happens to one in four college females and you and I are two in eight."

Stacey let that sink in a moment. Frankie began more tears.

"The fact that there are no signs of you fighting back lead me to believe you were drugged and completely out of it, non-consenting in the legal sense," Stacey continued.

"This is not going to go away with a couple of aspirin and the next great party. You'll live with it—as a part of you, who you are. You are a great kid, Frankie. With your whole life, well, you've heard all the bullshit 'life gives you lemons crap'. I want you to promise me one thing." Stacey was now the one in tears.

"Okay." Tears again and she was unable to speak.

"Promise me, you will tell someone. Promise me you will tell a friend, your mother, a counselor, or Blotto. You don't have to make a formal statement but you have to talk about it." Another long pause.

"You don't, and you'll find yourself telling a twenty-year old complete fucking stranger in about twelve years."

She embraced Frankie with a mother's bear hug and exhausted as she was, Frankie wanted this women to never let go.

"Wait. Are you sure I was...well... how do we know if I..."

"The triage nurse gave me what she learned. The doctor and I spent time piecing together your story; your symptoms, and once you'd agreed to the exam, we knew we were looking at a traumatic experience that you may or may not recall today, tomorrow, or next week. This discharge notice will spell out for you our findings. There appears to have been more than one instance of vaginal penetration, and an anal tear which appears to have resulted in penetration by either a very large penis or some other foreign object." She let that resonate with Frankie.

"But you need to understand that simply taking the 'morning after' pill seventy-two hours after a sexual encounter may or may not do the trick. More importantly, you need to take care of yourself physically and mentally for the next few weeks." She continued. "This is not about Thursday night anymore, Frankie. It's about *you* and getting *you* back to good."

"There is no good. I suck." Frankie was sobbing again. *How do I still have tears?* She'd been raped. She was torn and broken. *Just make it all stop.*

"You don't suck or you wouldn't be at Cal. If you were no good, you'd never have even thought about leaving your hometown. You wouldna made the curling squad, made the grades to get in here. You are a Golden Bear, Frankie. You are going to come out of this stronger and—fuck, I said I'd quit with all the bullshit—but you really are an amazing individual, who has recently suffered a bit of a drug-induced setback. You're gonna heal up, and you need to promise me you'll follow up. Follow up with me, or Renee, or someone you choose. I can guarantee you, of all the stories I have heard and shared, not one survivor I know of has had an easy road of it, but you'll get there." Silence and slow steady tears from both.

"Frankie. I want to thank you." Stacey extended her hand.

"What..." she instinctively shook as best she could.

"You got something out of me that had been locked away improperly for far too long, thank you. And think about that. You can do for others by helping Blotto shut that drugging shit down. I needed you. And I didn't know it. Renee needs you. Please."

"I can't..."

"You can, and you will." Stacey helped Frankie get her sweats on.

Stacey and Frankie exchanged mobile numbers. "Text anytime Frankie. I owe you one."

"I don't think I can do this." the voice was unrecognizable to her. She was a weak and filthy whore now; used and battered and a pathetic slut. She'd heard stories about 'girls like her.' It was now official, she was one of them.

Seated in the wheelchair, she honestly could not muster the will to stand. The two elders lifted her into the front seat and exchanged a look.

"I texted you her home address, Blotto. Keep me posted. Love you."

"Love you too, Stace. I'll call you after your shift." Blotto pulled away from the curb as Stacey let tears flow unabashedly.

The drive from Tang to Benvenue is less than four minutes, but seems like an hour of awkward silence to Frankie. As they pull up to the curb in front of her place, Blotto parks and stops the engine. *Hmmm how does this play out? I am NOT inviting her in.*

Blotto is out and around to Frankie's door in a flash.

"Let me help…"

"I can get out of the—" Wow. Her legs really do not seem to be answering her brain and moving at all. Realizing she's been holding her breath, she inhales deeply and tries again.

"Look. I'll just get you up the stairs and to your room. You need to rest." Blotto could read the fear and insecurity in this kids eyes.

167

"K. Well, I don't have my—" the door opened and two wide-eyed roomies stared out at the vehicle. Much as they 'barely knew this freak from the curling team,' they had now seen her brought home on two separate occasions by randos and curiosity had set in, to say the least.

"Hey," called one.

"Need some help?" asked the other.

"Nah. We're good." Blotto scooped up both legs and placed them on the curb then somehow got behind Frankie and lifted under her armpits.

"Damn. My legs are like noodles."

"It's the anesthetic not entirely worn off. Let's just get you to—"

"Yup. Thanks Renee. It's just up half a flight." *I'll be damned if I am gonna engage in conversation with less than month old roommates. Probably best to get past them and up as quickly as possible.*

It was an uneventful climb to her room, and seemingly simple task to drop her on the bed. *Bitch is strong for an old bag.*

As Frankie tossed back the IKEA feather comforter, the situation took a bit of a turn. There on the bed, wadded up in a ball, but *fire engine red* was a filthy silk *something.*

Sirens went off simultaneously for both—eyes turned on each other immediately.

Did she…oh shit.

What the fuck —is that a red dress? Blotto was unsure about wording here.

"Uh….I….when I got back….well, thanks for the ride."
Maybe she'll let it slide. Please, Frankie hoped.

"Sorry. No. I am not working today but yes, that is causing my internal radar to buzz on full fuckin alarm right now." *Blotto. Do not obtain evidence without proper procedure.*

"It's *not mine*." tears came without warning.

"Look. I am not saying it's *yours*, but let's be honest here. It…is…in…your room." *Careful Renee.* "Again. I am not on duty. And, well for fuck's sake."

"I have no idea how it got here. I swear. When I….I…it was Friday I think…well someone…that freak….that chick who brought me home the other day, maybe it's hers?" *Think Frankie. Think. WTF is it doing on your bed? Who was that dip that keeps popping up in my head?*

"Look. Let's take a breather here. Regroup." Blotto's mind racing like a freight train not stopping at the station.

"You mentioned some gal helped you home on Friday morning. Do you think she might be able to help us identify the owner of this here red…well, can you introduce us?"

"Seriously. I don't think you are hearing me. I don't even know her." *I do not WANT TO know her...or remind her of me in this fucking condition...I gotta remember something.*

"Well... I...shit...maybe I can show you where she lives."

"Have you got a paper bag kid*?" ...not leaving without this little pot o' gold.* "If it's not yours, you don't mind my takin it right?" *It's a gift. Given of free will. She can take it, right?*

"Kitchen." Frankie pointed and was relieved to see her leave the room. *What now?*

There is, of course, no clean paper bag to be found. She does her best to dump out the shit from the bottom of a Dollar Tree one— this needs to get to the lab ASAP. Do I call whatshishandle or drop it myself? She's deep in thought when Frankie appears almost presentable in jeans and a tee shirt ready to go.

"Hey. It's okay if you don't feel up to it." *Renee wants this red silk in straightaway.* "We can meet your friend another time."

"For fuck's sake, no one listens...it's *not* my friend. I don't even know her name, but I think I can get you to where she lives, k? Now. Let's go before I change my mind." *No fuckin way I am letting this cop think that's my dress for even one minute. This little do-gooder had better be home. Crap why can't I remember her name. Do I know her from somewhere?* All the jumbled recollections and fears are mounting. Time to clear this shit a bit, bitch better fuckin answer the door. *I really, really need a nap.*

Holly

Holly had early class on Monday morning, and her mind was all over the place since her unexpected visitors last night. *I have done zero reading. Please don't call on me today.*

What was that last night—did she actually apologize and ask me to be her friend? After the whole 'we never met' from Friday? What a difference a day makes is right.

But a police detective? Really this was getting out of hand, should she call her mom back and...no way, Mom will FUHREAK if I mention the cops are involved. Medical attention, great but cops?

Sunday evening Holly was expecting the Dominoes delivery man. When she got to the door with a couple of singles for the tip she was shocked at what she saw.

It was Frankie being helped up the stairs by some older lady, who frankly might as well have been a man. What the heck.

"Hey. Can I come in?" *Really?* Holly was too shocked to actually say anything.

"Hi. I'm Renee." *Well if she'd said Butch or Brett I'da wondered.*

"So then. Turns out my weekend is all about making new friends." Frankie tried to be jolly knowing she probably was less than friendly on their initial meeting(s).

Blotto stayed and took care of the pizza and tip—semi inviting herself in to ask Holly to provide a bit of background from the weekend that Frankie was fuzzy on.

171

No. Holly did not get the name or plate on Friday. Yes, Frankie had slept here on Friday night after the whole bump in at Derby.

Yes. Holly agreed it was likely some sort of drug or alcohol induced stupor she'd witnessed Friday morning, evening and all the way in to Saturday.

"I gave her ibuprofen is all on Saturday. She barely ate a thing. I honestly wondered about seeking medical attention but she was such a bit...so adamant about not being seen *with me or BY anyone.*" Holly was doing her best to help piece the seventy-two hours or so from Thursday late night through her attempt to find Frankie again on Saturday.

"Saturday was so much chaos with all the traffic and the tailgate parties. I tried to find you before and after the library but there was no answer at your place. Not even a roommate when I knocked and knocked."

Sunday morning she'd talked herself out of trying again being that Frankie was quite frank about them 'having never met' last they'd spoken.

Holly was helpful in providing a second witness of the timeline Blotto had worked out. Midnight red dresses, emergency transport of first victim at about one thirty am...where was Frankie during this time?

"No. I honestly don't remember her from the party. The first time I laid eyes on her she was basically passed out in the middle of

College Ave hanging out of her red...wait —" Holly stopped herself.

"She was wearing red on Friday morning, you think?" Blotto was feverishly taking notes.

"No. I don't even own a red towel." Frankie jumped in. "Red is literally *not allowed* on campus."

"If I am being completely honest, she wasn't actually 'wearing anything at all.' This red silk number was draped over or around her sorta. Let's face it, you were next ta naked there girl."

Incredibly uncharacteristically Frankie broke down in complete ugly cry mode. Wailing in fact.

Blotto and Holly took a moment to weigh before speaking.

"It's really not that odd ya know. I see naked girls walkin around campus *all the time*." Holly's attempt at humor failed.

Blotto came back from the bathroom with a wad of toilet paper in her hand. "No Kleenex. Never is in these parts."

A slight ease in the flow, followed by a wipe and a grin. "For fuck's sake, what are you two staring at?"

With that, tensions eased, conversation flowed with a fair amount of two on one. Frankie and Blotto pebbled Holly with questions. She did her best to answer from what little she knew as fact.

Asian guy helped. No key, but someone had left the door open. Dropped her to her place before noon, maybe as early as 11. Saw her next at Derby just after ten pm. Gaps in the timeline were determined to be 'sleeping it off,' which honestly still had not completed itself.

Frankie made an attempt at apologizing to Holly for any mistreatment. Blotto tossed in an apology of her own, admitting that without the dress, she was at a bit of a plateau in her investigation.

"Should this turn out to be Jessica's, well her *mother's* dress, I think we gotta get you two in the same room and see if there is any jogged memory from being in the same place at some point Thursday night."

"Not happening." Frankie had softened but remained adamant about not wanting to participate in any 'police business' or legal matter of any kind. *I seriously cannot let this one night woopsie daisy turn into a headline story.*

"I have an idea," *perky Holly, full of ideas.* "I take the dress over to the medical center and see if Jessica recognizes me —not that I feel drugged at all, but I'll be able to read her eyes right away if it's hers. Well her mom's dress anyways. That will help your case, won't it detective?" *Sheesh, now she's a junior detective. Frankie needed sleep.*

They agreed to leave the detective work to Blotto, and parted company. Blotto assured Holly, she'd be back in touch.

Frankie

Frankie was starting to get some strength back Sunday night. Recapping what she could recall. She'd made a to do list for the coming days: Sponge bath only for the first forty-eight hours—ick. Get some yogurt to take with the antibiotics—yuck. Maybe send a note to that nurse from Tang—Stacey something. It was nearly eight and a knocking on the door interrupted her thoughts.

"Frankie. I know you're in there. I saw you go in." *female voice, cannot place it.*

"Come on, Frankie. I don't want things to be awkward between us." *still nothing.*

"Frankie. It's me, Marla. Let me in. I KNOW you're in there." *Marla who?*

"Look. It's not my fault Coach put me in the foursome. I don't even like curling. I swear, if it bothers you, I will quit." *Quit. Who's quittin what?*

"I mean it, Frankie. I'll quit." *This person was not taking silence for an answer.*

"Can I help you?" as Frankie opened the door she realized she'd seen this person somewhere before but couldn't place her. "Quit what? Do you maybe have a wrong number?"

"Wrong number? I am trying to apologize Frankie. Coach put me on the squad, without even good reason. I mean missing one practice. If I missed a practice no one would even care and now for some reason you hate me."

"Whoa, whoa, whoa slow down. What are you talking about?" *Ah, Marla the Transfer. No idea what she's talking about.*

"Look. I get it. Coach is just trying to make an example—" *Marla has the most annoying squeak of a voice.*

"Ok. Lemme stop you right there. I saw Coach this morning and he said nothing about the squad—frankly your teeny bopper voice is killing me. Come in, sit down." *Can I get ONE minute of peace today?*

"No seriously, I will quit. I hate curling, my dad made me—"

"Hold on, hold on. No one actually *likes* curling. Let's start from the top. Remind me your name?"

"Oh my gawd, of course. You have no idea who I am. I'm Marla."

"Ah. Yes. Marla the Transfer. Do you have a last name? Have we formally met before right here right now? What are you yappin' about with my squad?"

"Marla. Marla Thomas."

"You're kidding me, right? Marla, not Marlo Thomas?" *Mom was always watching old sit coms. Mom. OhmyGod, I didn't call home today. Shit. Mom. What am I gonna say to her? Shit. Nothing. Say nothing. Dammit. I completely forgot our Sunday call.*

176

"Just a sec." Frankie grabbed her phone off the kitchen counter and unplugged the charger from its butt. *Home button, phone, favorites...'she who must not be named.' Damn. I should change that.*

"Mom. Hey Mom. Really, really sorry I forgot to call earlier but my friend Marla is here. Can I call you tomorrow?"

"Yes. No. Yes, you'll meet her when I see you at Regionals. Yes. Okay. Thanks Mom, me too.*" Seems so cheeky to spit out 'love you' when someone else is in the room.*

"Okay. Where were we?"

"I really am sorry, Frankie."

"Sorry for what?" *Sheesh.* She'd improved a bit on the squeak but what does this girl want outta me?

"Look. I heard what happened...and..."

"Wait. What? Wait just a Goddamn minute. You heard what?" *Honestly not remembering shit is startin' to piss me off.*

"Well. It's not my place to—"

"What the fuck are you talking about?" *Keep it cool. See what she says, or saw.*

Suddenly Marla is sobbing. Frankie is losing her patience. Jane hadn't said two words. A and B were not answering her texts.

"K. Stop crying and tell me what you heard."

"I'm sorry. Its just that—"

"It's just what?" *Spit it out.*

"Well. It's just that...I was raped too. That's why I transferred."

Wait. What the fuck? Who said anything about rape?

"What are you talking about?"

"People said—" wiping her nose on her arm.

"What people? Start from the beginning." Frankie was trying her best to not let on but her heart rate was thru the roof.

"At practice Friday. People were talking about a party and you, and maybe some guy. I don't know. They weren't talking to me. I just overheard some stuff."

"Tell me exactly what you heard, Marlo?" *Damnitalltohell.*
"Mind if I call you Marlo?"

Holly

At the end of the Sunday discussion, Holly had agreed to allow Frankie a bit of leeway on the initial meet and greets because of the drug screening results. They would actually be grabbin Pete's later on this week they'd decided. Maybe a new friend after all.

Blotto had shared some of that information about the drugs with Holly, but honestly she knew very little about it all, aside from aspirin and Tylenol were for pain.

The words date and rape were two that neither she nor Frankie had used on their earlier discussions, and Holly was so thankful that she'd actually gone for medical help. She secretly wondered which of the Boater boys may have been involved in getting Frankie—well, offering her punch—that really was quite a party.

She'd called her mother with the update at about ten her time, nearly one am in Florida, and her mother was thankful too. "You see dear. You are doing the lord's work out there. This poor lost soul had no one else to turn to. Even the most popular kids feel lonely now and again without the Holy Spirit in their hearts. Take her with you on Wednesday to your small group."

"Mom. I told you fourteen times, she doesn't want to talk to anyone about it. I shouldn't even be telling *you*. The only reason she even came to me is because I could provide some of the details she couldn't remember about how she got home and stuff. It's not like we're besties now." *A friend still the same. Holly was geeked.*

"All I am saying is thank the lord you were raised to do the right thing, Holly. Tables turned, well, I mean, there have been stories here in our parish of young ladies off at college forgetting. Well, I am so happy that you are making friends is all. Just be sure the friends you're making are...well, well be sure they're making good choices too is all I ask. I love you, Hollyhoney."

"Mom. Let me interrupt you right there. Not a word to *anyone*, especially not at church. This person came by and told me she got help—I was just filling you in so that you could hear that 'you

179

were right as usual' again. Okay? Happy? Sorry. I woke you up for this."

"Honey, you call me anytime, day or night, I love you. God Bless You. Now, you get some sleep too, dear." Mom was sleep talking, it was only ten west coast time. She knew Holly was a night owl.

"Night, Mom." but she'd already hung up the phone.

Well, that's that. Friends? Nope, not buyin' it. We'll see if she texts me this week. That girl has a bunch of popular girls for friends on her team, frankly I am fine with that. I need study time, not a bunch of new friends.

But that was the most sensational weekend ever imaginable for sure. First picking her up outta the street, then Derby. Who woulda thunk she'd be showing up at my door with a cop. Maybe Wednesday I can work in an hour or two of research on those drugs Frankie took—well, had in her. Wow. What if I had had a cup of punch that night? Holy moly...the lord works in mysterious ways.

Blotto

Sunday evening, after hours, Blotto should *not* be pulling in to the building. Even before she could take the turn off of MLK, she saw his car—*fuckin Feinstein, always tryna one up somebody. Shit, it'll have to wait.*

She drove past and hit CVS for a bottle of Jameson to take the edge off. Get a clean paper bag while she's there. It was very likely this red number had seen a few swaps the past few days, but damned if she was gonna lose credibility over the fact that it's not bagged when she is able to turn it in.

Headed home, she texted Stacey. "WYA." their shortcut for where you at.

'Your place. Out back. Since when did you start locking your porch door?' They'd been friends so long they both remembered the days when no one ever locked the garage or back door. Both sets of parents had survived Berkeley in the 60s without so much as house keys on their hemp woven rings.

"13." Renee would be home in thirteen minutes.

Stacey smiled at the fact that some things never changed.

Since preteen days, Renee always chose odd numbers for her ETA—never 10, 15, or half hour—always 7, 19, or in this case 13. They'd been able to read each other's minds and secret code texts since way before LOL hit mainstream. Her mind took her back to the day they'd had to explain to their moms, at separate houses, flawlessly that LOL was love you lots without having previously discussed it. That brought an audible laugh.

"What's so funny?" Renee's window down in the Prius. She snuck up the driveway without a sound and caught Stacey laughing.

"Nothing really. Long day. How's the patient?"

"Which one? I honestly feel like I need to see a doctor."

"Me too." Stacey was pensive. "Look, I never told you because—"

"I knew. You didn't have to tell me. Reminder Stace, I know you better than you know you. That whole bullshit line about needing girl time—we never once did girl shit."

"Only because I knew you'd never ever admit."

"Fuck you."

"Fuck you too. So did she give you anything for your case?" Stacey was hopeful that Renee had gotten Frankie to open up a bit.

"Get this." grabbing a Blue Moon from the six pack on the patio table. "She's got a red dress at her place." Renee let that set for a spell while she downed nearly the entire beer. "Red dress. Cal student. Not exactly your run o' the mill Dress Barn number but looks to be an authentic Dolce & Gabbana little number, like money."

"You don't think?" Stacey asked, wide-eyed.

"I don't have to think, *I know* that our vic at the med center is *missing* one high-end little red dress, my friend. Shit's gettin' weird." She finished the first and grabbed for another. "And some little church-goer gave me quite a story about Frankie having it either draped on or wrapped around her on Friday morning—no way she'd fit in the damn thing. It's a size two."

"No one I know fits in a two, but I gather that's not really the point." they both laugh and pick up the beers to head inside.

"Hungry?" Renee asks.

"Famished. But the beer's doing a nice job of holding me over til you can whip something up if that's what you're askin." Stacey made fun of Renee's desire to be in the kitchen all their growing up years, but turns out she maybe shoulda been payin closer attention.

"I already had a slice, but I gotta get my greens. Cut these strawberries before you get too drunk." Renee tossed the plastic pint, Stacey missed the thing and it popped open on the linoleum floor. "Well shit fire, wash 'em too."

Over a spinach salad the two talked about today, last year, high school and beyond. Such a close friendship and so many words unspoken between them. The issue of Renee not having been in any sort of relationship yet, and Stacey having been in and out of too many, stayed locked in their hearts with a safety key needing no words. Full understanding without words. A genuinely grand find in a friendship.

What they didn't talk about was their own run-ins with assailants. Renee having hospitalized a guy that tried to get too frisky senior year; Stacey asking for a pick-up from Planned Parenthood that first summer after high school. They knew each other well enough to let some things slide. *Don't sweat the small stuff, and chill on the big stuff.*

"Where do you think the dress will take you?" *let's avoid the sexual assault and medical aspects for a spell.*

"Honestly, with the FBI now involved, I may have to simply hand it over and let it be. My guess is without charges being filed by the Stanford gal, they may even give it back to her, *as is*, I might add. Hideousness."

"Oh gawd...does it stink?"

"Haven't really given it the Febreeze test, but from the looks of it, *'well worn.'* The kid described it as 'brand new with tags on' from the start of the night. I cannot even imagine how it got to this level of filth—don't want to think about it in fact. And who the fuck pays twelve hundred for a dress these days? Don't they know about H&M for cripes sake?"

More light laughter and avoidance of the core issues. Renee grabbed a clean sheet and pillow case to set up the couch for Stacey.

"Only three beers a piece but by God you are not getting a DUI on my watch. Plus, I got a Jameson needing tending to, you want it with soda or straight up?"

"Neat and tidy. Here. Let me do the couch. You get the whiskey."

It was nearly midnight when Renee climbed the stairs to her room. "Stacey, I love you, you know that right? Not like love you, but you are my person, k? Don't ever change."

"Love you too RayRay, get some sleep. And thanks. Thanks for taking this on for me—means a lot."

Once situated on the couch, Stacey felt the tears well up again. *Can anyone save us all?*

Renee propped herself up for the nightly ritual. Being near the back of a notebook always made the journaling more difficult, but tonight the kink was from an entirely different source. *How many women will it take for a change?* She'd read *The Tipping Point* by Malcolm Gladwell years ago and had been certain she'd seen more than a dozen 'points.' Lady Gaga's video did virtually nothing to end rape on campuses. The streets of San Francisco becoming more and more dangerous. Number one public university simply looking the other way on nearly every case on or off campus. What to say? What to write? What to do?

She slid the book into the nightstand with nothing more than the date and an over-sketched broken heart symbol she'd scrolled. No words. She gently tugged on the chain on the bedside lantern and pulled the feather tick up. She'd had only four hours sleep in the last three days.
Goodnight Moon and Stars. She was out.

PART V

MONDAY

Headline: *UCPD issue second alert investigating alleged assault at Barge*

An individual was sexually assaulted on campus early Friday morning, according to a UCPD alert released the same day. The alert did not specify the victim's affiliation with the campus, but did confirm this is a second alert today. Late on Thursday night, the victim met three suspects, the first of which she knew from a previous encounter, at the Barge on Piedmont. Sometime after eleven pm Thursday night, and into the morning hours Friday, the suspects assaulted the victim multiple times. They allegedly sexually assaulted the victim just after her escort left her on the dance floor at a party in the building. The victim, unconscious for most of Friday, did not contact the police but reported the incident to multiple witnesses. According to the UCPD crime alert, the suspects are described as: Suspect No. 1 — A Hispanic or white male, 6-foot2 in height, 19 to 21 years of age with a medium build, dark eyes, and collar-length, curly brown hair; wearing a baseball cap and nothing else. Suspect No. 2 — A white male, approximately 6-foot in height, in his 20s, with a medium build and wearing nothing at all. Suspect No. 3 – A white male, approximately 5-foot-9, obesely overweight with red hair, also wearing nothing at all. Anyone with any information is encouraged to contact UCPD Detective Monroe at 510-640-0000 from 8 a.m. to 5 p.m.

@MsThang: No means No. Just don't go ain't a fix. #endrapeoncampus

@JD: Law should protect the victim, not the University #rapehappenswhenUCBlookstheotherway

@Annon: Bitch asked for it – spin cycle rules. #longlivethebarge

@Sporty: Fun catching up w/ @calmensfball saw @RealKidd last night. Looking forward to his induction into the @CalAthletics #HOF in December

Cal Athletics

"Okay folks, successful weekend." Willard was addressing the middle and upper management staff in the department. "There was a ton of baloney flying around amongst the kids, but I think overall the alumni were pleased with the barbecue skewers and bobble heads."

He looked around the table but no one was giving feedback. In fact, staffers seemed to be not paying any attention at all. "What the hell folks. You gonna say you didn't like the Marshawn Lynch bobbleheads?

"Sir. I think the elephant in the room—" Andrea started but was interrupted.

"It's a full-blown legal team taking us on from the other side of the pond there, sir." Assistant Martin Moore had been on board through too many of these assault cases not to notice that this one was very different in size and scope.

"They are *suing the University*, sir, not the frat house."

"Nice of you to show up *'Martin who disappears on Fridays, Moore'*. I won't bother asking where the fuck you were, and who put you in charge of *legal check-ups* this week? I have our team on it."

Willard really had no desire to delve into the barge issue with this group; it was entirely up to the Greeks and the lawyers as far as he was concerned.

"Now then. Did everyone meet their development goals? Andrea. Why don't you give us the financial update." *Not today. It's Monday and I will not let those Stanford pricks and their little legal threats kill this wave of enthusiasm over the Lynch visit and bobble head. Marshawn had brought his mother of all people, our lead story for the magazine this quarter.*
Bitchin!

Beau

Monday morning Beau was awakened by the bling of a text message. *Damn. Forgot to put it on do not disturb.*

"CMM." Oh *lord.* Call Me Maybe *from Frankie.* The last person on earth he cared to talk to was her.

He rolled over, pulling the pillow over his head with him. Unable to get back to sleep, he recalled how bothered he'd been by her constant begging, texting, and naked selfies. All of that had subsided since Thursday night. *What the fuck did he ever do to her?*

And *fuck her* for fucking fuckin around with fuckin *Dewey.* Jesus. He missed Brandy like never before. *What time is it back home? Damn. She's still at school.* He flipped the switch to silent mode and dove back under the covers deeper.

Dewey

Dewey was getting dressed for breakfast with the folks. It had been a very shocking couple of days to say the least, seeing his mother roll up mid-day Saturday and drag him by the earlobe to her vehicle. They'd gone together to bail Dad outta the tank. The ride back to Fresno was completely silent, and Sunday was not much different aside from his mother droning on to his dad about what a disappointment he was. He could just hear through the wall...*wanted better for her children...setting examples...not just do better next time, be a better man this time.* Pops sure was getting a licking.

He looked down at this twitter feed. Rumors were flying on social media about the house being shut down. Police investigation. Two victims; no names to report.

Far as he could comprehend, Dad and a few of his buddies had a bit of a scuffle over parking Saturday, and Mom had had to miss the quilt show all weekend on accounta the arrest and what not. Wonder what's the what.

Sure was good to be home for some home cooking though. Sunday dinner was amped up with his being home and all.

Not a good time to tell 'em about my maybe having a new girlfriend LOL. He did have fond memories though. *Thursday night was sort of a blur, but that silk dress Friday morning, damn she was one fine ass 'lady in red.' Dude, hope Beau ain't fired up about it all. He's got plenty a women.*

Monday morning back at the precinct:

"Look, Blotto, we got no one pressing any charges. I like the little red number you got there, but we are not participating in some sort of soap opera *whose dress is it anyways* caper. Drop it." Chief was only using his mild, change my mind if you can voice.

"We have two separate victims, unknown to one another but at the same party, both showing high levels of GHB and Rohypnol in their blood stream. Vic 2 was seventy-two hours out from ingestion, this is a huge deal, sir."

Blotto had obtained all she could from the medical staff at BMC, and Frankie handed over her entire 'packet' from the checkout clerk. Levels that high seventy-two hours post-ingest screamed of overdose potential, potentially lethal.

So it wasn't exactly fair how she'd obtained it. Frankie was refusing to go on record, but she had said that Blotto could 'copy it or shred it.' Her choice. The dress was happily 'donated,' when Frankie realized its possible origin.

"We got a bunch of drunk co-eds time and time again. This. The GHB. This we gotta shut down and quick. Lucky as hell no one—that we know of—has overdosed on this shit."

Chief Orzo had been thinking much the same about the level of drug use escalating within the city limits of late. Aside from the usual student partiers, meth-heads had become a steady stream of violent offenders on his watch.

Maybe if he were to give Blotto a special assignment, she could dig out the actual dealer the kids were buying off of. 2016 being an election year; a nice big drug bust on his watch would make for a bit of decent PR for a change.

"Take Jones, get back out there to the barge and see if anyone is still living there. If so, let's try to cut a deal with the kids. They set us up an appointment with their supplier. We go a bit lighter on the shutdown, like maybe it's still inhabitable but parties banned or something. Work with that Greek leader from Cal, and take one of our undercovers to work in on the deal. You've got three days. Full report to me by Wednesday then we regroup. Clear?"

"Yessir. Yes. And thanks, Chief, you will not be disappointed." Blotto was on a mission. Not exactly a blank check, but some newly allocated resources and really good leads.

"Wait. The dress. Can I deliver it to the Stanford vic so I can at least get her reaction? Pretty damn sure it's hers, but maybe the sight of it will get her talking."

"Look, Blotto. I am not about to step on any toes. Does anyone else know about the damn thing at this point?" Orzo knew she was right, and frankly the FBI was not pushing very hard being that the vic wasn't pressing charges.

"No, sir. Well." in her head she could only think of this kid Holly muddying up if anyone were to find her. Blotto had kept her name out of her report so far.

"No, sir. I did not mention it to any law enforcement nor log it in to evidence just yet. With no pending case, maybe we simply 'return to owner' if word gets out. But I would like to have it tested. Shit. What do you think, boss?"

"Again. Don't go sniffing up any extra work, Blotto. Get 'er done." Sheesh, just the hint of a 'tampering with evidence' could blow up in his face big time on this deal.

Frankie

Frankie woke Monday confused on so many levels. She rubbed the sleep out of her eyes and stretched. *OUCH. God it hurts to move*.

The previous few days were finally coming in to some sort of muddy lucidity. Clear in that she was forever changed. Assaulted, violated, soiled, ruined, trodden amongst frat boys. Basically white trash. Tears flowed. Self-loathing set in. Frankie, of last week, was officially invaded by this battered, bruised, and used piece of shit. *I can't. I just cannot stand it anymore. Make it be a bad dream, please.*

A few weeks ago, hell even just a few days ago, she'd been on top of the world. Benching 140, 17 on the beep, she and Jane were unstoppable on the ice; A and B having trained in other countries had broom skills unseen in these parts. They'd take Regionals and move on for certain. Now what?

Coach never did text or check on her after the drop Sunday morning. Should she initiate? Was Marla really tapped to replace her? If so, how come Coach said nothing yesterday? *Probably the look of me distracted him.*

Beau wasn't blowing up her phone either. *Dammit why did she even send the CMM this morning?* She surely was not ready to see him, or anyone just yet. Were they still a 'thing'? Were they *ever* really a thing or was it only in her mind?

She glanced over at her mirror where she had written in lipstick YOLO in swirly script lettering. *Ha.*

195

Corny AF. She first laid eyes on Beau and began shopping bride magazines in her head. All the clichéd shit; shooting stars, heart palpitations, babies, two golden bears make cubs, a golden future. All of this the very first coffee date.

He'd said he had 'never met anyone exactly like her.' That she was a *'one in a million, outta the ballpark, winner of a chicken dinner.'* Chopped liver now. Her big life chapter and happily ever after had been just within reach. How could she possibly recover from this?

Using every bit of energy to will herself upright and into the bathroom, she popped the blister pack of ibuprofen mid-pee. First pill dropped in the toilet. *Can't fuckin do anything right anymore.* Hands shaking, tears flowing. *I so just wanna kill myself. Wait. What...really... do I? Oh for fuck's sake, hopeless and alone. I suck sooo bad. So fuckin cliché, fuckin suicidal.* She didn't think she could feel any lower until she saw the illumination of her iPhone on the edge of the sink.

FTFO. Fuck. The. Fuck. Off.

The text message was from Beau. *It's over. He knows. Wait. Did he...he HAS to answer me.*

Call me you mother fucker. NOW. Her thumbs couldn't be fast enough.

No answer. *Calling his ass.* Ten rings, no answer.

"Fuck You."

"Hey. You okay in there?" roommate musta heard that one.

"Yeah. Cool. Just dropped an Advil in the tank." *Nice one.*

"I got the Costco size out here. Help yourself. They're on the counter. Peace out."

Frankie heard the front door open and close. Alone. Class or no go. One more peek in the mirror made the decision for her. She climbed back into bed and cued up New Girl on the iPad. *Fuck that student athlete shit. Jess wasn't athletic and she survives.*

Bling. Her phone. She hopped back to the toilet in a flash, hoping. Mandatory Meeting 4pm PDC. It was Coach.
Fuck me harder. Not. Going.

She took her phone back to bed with her, before pulling the covers up—bling—maybe.

FRANKIE MY OFFICE 3:45. Coaches text to just she.

Fuck it. I will go in to drop my gear. I QUIT.

Beau

Beau didn't have a twitter handle, nor did he want one, but the buzz today was killing him. Was he involved? Who was the girl? Was she gonna cry rape? Ambulance, police, shutting down the Barge. Topics a plenty.

He was almost inside the building and determined a divisive text was necessary and PDQ. *Shit. What did I put her in my phone as...HOTBD, TuTh, BB6...wait, she texted me. Oh yeah HTQT4...three prior hit & quits.* He laughed.

FTFO. Fuck. The. Fuck. Off.

That should do it. He pranced into psych 201 refreshed, settled, confident...until he saw that chick in the third row; if eyes could kill. *WTF is she lookin at?*

Row 4 and 6, all eyes on him. *Fuck this shit. Beau out.* He turned and headed to the rec center. An easy game of pick up always going in rec sports gym. *Fuckin Whore.*

Now, she's calling. *Fuckin power down. No way bitch. I barely touched ya.* He tossed the iPhone into his backpack and picked up the pace.

John

John had been laying low most of Saturday and Sunday. The whole boats not being assigned on Friday, hoopla of the FOAM party Saturday before the debilitating loss to Oregon —he'd lost a hundred bucks betting on that shit. Then Sunday reading a few @s about the Barge being shut down. Sure was glad he'd decided to get his own place this year.

Up and out early Monday morning he hit the gym. No class til eleven on Mondays—what kinda dork took eight am classes *any* day much less on a Monday?

The rec center was hopping. Mondays filled up with all the wanna-bes thinking they'd start a routine 'this week,' never failed there'd be lines for machines only on Mondays. As he waited for the leg machine, he overheard a few separate conversations, not that he was eavesdropping but common threads were rape, ambulance, police, boaters, Barge and BEAU. *Shit. I haven't seen him much this weekend. He go all offline with that Brunette after all?*

John dipped into his bag and grabbed for his Beats; just some Drake this morning thank you very much, enough bullshit about the Barge. Pumpin iron made the world outside simmer down and his reflection amp up. *Gotta post up a mirror in my room for am sit ups—damn, I'm looking swole.*

He was feeling much better after ninety minutes of pain for gain. Now. For a heathy snack. Jamba was just over and up a block or two.

"Dude, whaddup?" John was leaving as Beau was fumbling for his ID card. "Dude, he's cool." motioning for the squirrel behind the desk to let Beau in.

"Oh. I know *very well* who he *is*, but you don't get in without ID," snapped the clerk.

Beau stared right into the eyes of the clerk. "Fuck you. You don't know me man."

"Yo. Maybe we grab a Jamba?" John at that point noticed Beau was just a bit off his game this morning. "I gotta gift card. I gotchu man."

"Got somethin ta say. Say it to my face, shitforbrains."

"Okay. Okay. Let's hit it." John tugs at Beau's arm but he's not budging.

"No. Fuck you, you little shrimp. Who the fuck died and made you king?" Losing his temper was not the norm for him but damnit the jeers and snickers were starting to get to him.

"King not. Court Jester maybe. I sure don't need to muscle up some bae to get bizzy widdit." The clerk was quite pleased with himself, and confident only in that there was a four foot high locked desk between them—and his beefy supervisor just through the glass window across.

"What the—"

John grabbed with both hands and dragged Beau out onto the courtyard off Bancroft. "Listen, dude. Don't...you can't let them get to ya."

"Bullshit. Fuckin' bullshit. That bitch gets lit and I gotta get the looks?" Beau is convinced that Frankie must have dropped a dime to the cops or some shit. "Did you fuckin' know the cops showed up at my place Friday? Some bullshit."

"Wait, what? I saw you Friday. What the fuck are you talking about?" John was confused. He'd seen Beau Saturday and Sunday at the PDC as well—he'd never once mentioned talking to the cops. "Fuckinay man. Let's get that Jamba and talk it out." *Fuck. Fuck. Fuck. Did he mention my name to the cops?*

Edgar

Edgar had spent the better part of the weekend devising a plan. First, ditch the drugs. Be sure that the GroupMe was read and deleted by everyone. Find a couch to sleep on until the heat subsided at the barge. No way can they simply put a dozen guys out on the street over some stupid party.

"Baker. Listen man. I gotta crash here again tonight. The heat be all up in the barge tearing shit up."

"I heard they got a CSI unit over there like some Hollywood movie n shit."

"Dude. Some serious shit is goin down. They fuckin taped shit off. Sounds like the big guys didn't get their tailgate in," adds Laskey. "Never caught up with my pops but he sounded pissed AF. Fuckin Dewey got dragged out by his Ma Saturday and I ain't seen him since."

"Fuckin' Dewey had better keep his mouth shut." Edgar knew that was an impossible wish. "He fuckin had last dibs and was supposta get the bitch home."

"What? I heard she waddin in no shape to go no place." Baker had left before the cops showed, but recalled a visual of Raul tryna keep a brunette upright on the dancefloor. "Was that bitch you were grinding on E? How the fuck did you get her up the stairs even? Had yourself a whole handful when I saw ya's."

"Fuck you, Baker. You never saw me with Frankie, you hear me?" Sweat beads instantly appeared on Edgar's forehead. "I told the cops I had no ladies, no how on Thursday night. Let's stick to the fuckin story, man." Wiping his brow he added, "Now. Let's go over it again— Beau brought her, Dewey slept with her, that's it. No added shit."

Raul couldn't help himself. "But fuckin' John had her doggy-style on two. How the fuck you gonna say she got to three on her own? Bitch was fuckin' sleep walkin' or some shit."

"Dammit, you two. How many times I gotta repeat myself? Beau brought her, Dewey did her—that's all we know—nobody saw *nothing*. Fuckin morons." Edgar had not caught up with Beau or John, and these two were of no use whatsoever. "If the fuckin cops wanna talk, you saw fuckin nuttin." He slammed the door on his way out.

"You're welcome. Stay again sometime soon," hollered Baker at the back of the door. "Raul, no shit, this is startinta look like it's every man for his self n shit. E be fuckin' tossin' Beau and Dew under the bus like that."

"Fuck him. I fuckin' hate when he goes all commando n shit. I hit that spin cycle out back, never saw Beau's bitch —but fuck if I am talkin' to any coppers. Deny 'til I die bastards. Whatchu got to settle my nerves?"

Raul was thinking more about the red dress and that hideous arm all bone out and flipped upside down that night. Reminded him of an exposed broken leg in a basketball final he saw on TV. Kept playing over and over in his mind. A toke or two would quell his nausea.

Baker came outta the kitchen with a lit bong and two Budweisers. "Hit power then cable on that mothah will ya?" Sunday afternoons were for ESPN and chillin.

After a coupla hits he grabbed for his cell phone. Raul was on his 'favorites' screen. "Make sure the pledges keep their mouths shut." And after no reply, "LOL. We are not goin' down for this shit."

John and Beau

John ordered two Berrywonders with a boost and sat back out on the curb with Beau to wait for their order. "So wassup man. Where you been?"

"Fuckinay. Bitch musta told the cops my name or some shit. Fuckin draggin me down to the station Friday for nothin. Fuckin blow job. I gotta fuckin quick hummer then headed home; fuck we had trials Friday morning. My ass was in bed no later than midnight Thursday night.
Some bullshit. Where the fuck were you Thursday night?"

"Thursday? Was that the party at the barge..." stuttering...

"Fuck you man. Of course it was. Fuckin spent all afternoon shootin' hoops and talkin' about it you asshole. Where the fuck were you?" Feeling the weight of the load.

Where the hell were all his guys the past few days? Not one dude had the decency to give him the straight story 'bout what went down after he left.

"You got Edgar's GroupMe right?" John still sounding like a girl. "I hit delete after I read it and all like you said, but sounds like somebody got hurt."

"*Hurt?* Fuckin paper said someone was transported by ambulance mothah fucker. What the fuck. And *no*, I did *not* get a fuckin text. What the fuck?"

John took a deep breath as he recalled the gist of the GroupMe. Beau brought her. Dewey did her. "Hey man. It ain't no big thang—this too shall pass."

"What the fuck, John. Don't give me that passive ass bullshit. Who freakin' ran the spin cycle? And who the fuck was out back on the fuckin' mattress-land fortress of fucking STD's for fuck's sake? Assholes. No fucking GroupMe. No email."

John's eyes gave him away.

"Fuckinay. There was an *email*?" This was bigger than he originally figured. *How dare they leave him out of the thread? He's fuckin actin-Barge Prez right now, ya bastards.*

"Let's go." Beau was up and dragged John by his bag strap.

"Wait. Where to?"

Sniveling idiot, thought Beau.

"Dude, my Jamba." John was not leaving without ten bucks worth of smoothie.

"You got a fuckin juice box at your place, asshole; you're gonna boot up and show me the email."

A cute little Jamba Juice clerk caught up with them before Urban Outfitters "Your Berrywonders, sir." She blushed. "You almost forgot." She was out of breath from running to catch them.

"Uh thanks. Thank you. I mean, well..."

"He means thanks. Let's go bro." Beau wasn't stopping for anyone or anything.

Neither of them took even one sip before they reached John's place up Bancroft. He had a small room off the back of an older house; no formal kitchen or office space, but a small desk set up with his laptop and a printer. Beau charged to it and slammed the Jamba down so hard the top popped off, juice splattering everywhere.

"Come on man, that's my keyboard. Lemme get—"

"Fuck you. Boot it up." Beau was uninterested in the fact that he may have just shorted out the box he was ordering John to power up.

"It's on you asshole. Sure hope it works after you just fuckin' juiced it." John wasn't worried a sliver about the Macbook, more-so about whether or not he'd properly deleted the email and emptied the trash all the way.

"Get me to recently deleted shit." Beau was enraged. Now frustrated by the fact that it was a MAC, and frankly he barely knew how to turn one on much less search for shit. *Why the fuck would anyone buy a MAC these days? PCs were a walk in the park. Lines out the door at the Apple Store tells ya'all ya need to know about 'customer support.' Fuck this fucker.* "Where's the trash icon?" he demanded.

"Lemme sit there man." John's heart was beating so thunderous he was worried Beau could hear it.

Edgar

"Look, man. If you read it, you know that it's nothing bad on you bro. All's I said was Beau brought her, Dewey did her—keepin' it 100, that's the haps. Not one person, including you, my friend, is gonna say she didn't show up askin' for some lovin."

Edgar could not believe this wicked streak. *How in hell did Beau get that email?* "And the cops don't give a fuck about the girls. They be all hot n bothered about the GHB— that's defs not our department. Fuckin chill, man."

"Fuckin chill? That's what you got, you motha fucker. Fuckin' hackin' into the Gmail and sendin' code behind mah back. Fuck you, E. You're history. I can't wait to see how you tryta get outta this shitshow—you know the rules, man. No one. No one fuckin' sends shit on me and thinks he can get away with it."

Beau did a bit of asking around the day before and heard the barge was as good as shut down so his threats were weak. He knew what he had to do—the detective's card was back at his place.

He tossed what was left of the juice onto the floor and headed for the door.

"Beau, straight up. No idea you actually liked her."

"Are you fucking kidding me right now?" Beau slammed the door hard enough to wake the neighbors.

Beau

Beau stormed out of the door on a mission. *Fuck these mother fucking 'brothas.' Not one gonna fess up or get with me on this shit. Truth's coming out and I am done. Won't know what hit 'em when I'm through singing to the cops. Fuck if I'm goin' down for this shit. Fuckin druggie motha fuckers and their bitches.*

He felt eyes on him the entire way. Like a fuckin fender bender they refuse to look away. *Nothin to see here folks. Show's about to start though. Druggies, bullshit team mates, and loser coaches. Fuck them all.*

As he rounded the corner of Dana and Derby, he saw her perched upon his stairs. *Mother-fuckin whore.*

His initial instinct was to dip, but too late, eyes met. *Wait. What? She's gotta black eye. Damn. She looks evil struck.*

"Yeah. Wassup, Frank?"

His demeanor immediately changed. Unlike tinmen bastard types, he did have a heart. "Are you ok and all?"

Dammit. I was not gonna cry. "Look Bo—"

"Holdup. Let's go inside. You need a Kleenex or some shit?" he didn't recognize his own voice, and for some reason his hands were shaking tryna engage the key.

After a long silence, toilet paper substitution for Kleenex. Two mostly clean glasses for water. Frankie spoke first. "Honest. I have not talked to the police...well, not officially anyways."

"What is that supposed to mean, Frankie? I barely touched you. What the fu—"

"You did *nothing*. That much I remember...I think. It's just —" she couldn't finish. She swore she wouldn't cry. "It's like I...well, I don't...can't... What the hell happened that night, Beau?" She broke into a million pieces.

"Geez. Stop cryin' will ya?" instinct kicked in and he held her while her body shuddered up and down back and forth with sobs.

Sure he was pissed off at the guys. Yes, this fumbling bundle of waterworks was the catalyst, but a switch sorta flipped in that moment.

This is some nasty ass way to live out my college days, different day, different issues but most of it not measuring up to expectations. He had come to Cal with ambitions other than hittin' one hundred pots o' honey. He'd been raised to respect and honor his mother and sister. So why was he tryna set some sort of record with these girls he had no interest in? *There was the thrill of the chase. Wait. No. That's part of the problem. There was no pursuit.*

Frankie composed herself somewhat. "Look. I just need you to tell me what happened Thursday, at the party. Why did you leave me?" her attempts to use her big girl voice were failing her and she knew she sounded like a sniveling idiot. "We...well, I thought we—"

"We didn't." Beau snapped back into reality. He did not have sex with this girl.

"Right. Well. I wondered what you remember...like what time and where did you leave me?"

"Uh...I went for a drink. *You* left *me*."

"Okay. Right. But after that...did we...did we dance, or how exactly did I get—"

"Look. I came back to the porch you were gone. I nabbed you off the dance floor and we fooled around a little bit in the john on two for a while. Not much. Well, you gave... let's just say we didn't have sex, okay?" Beau felt a stir below at the memory.

"Yeah, okay. So, on two...then what?" Frankie was too embarrassed to admit that she'd found herself on the third floor the next morning and hoped that Beau could help her find out how she got there.

209

"You were singing some oldies tune and took off on me back to the dance floor with your girls. I got cleaned up. Well you know...and by the time I got back to the first floor you were grinding all up on Edgar on the dance floor." He tried not to sound too judgey. "It really wasn't that big a deal and all. But I wasn't gonna butt in on that shit. We had trials the next day—which I told you when I invited you that I was leaving early—and I headed out. It just didn't seem like the right time to say any goodbye 'cause you were not ready to leave...you made that perfectly clear."

"What'd I say?"

"Shit if I know. You were mostly working the floor so hard I kinda figured you were just not that into me. Had to be about ten forty five cause I was home by eleven.

"Ten forty five. Then what happened?"

"That's exactly what I'd like to know." Looking at her made him cringe just as his gut gurgled audibly. "Uh sorry. Haven't eaten. You want some toast?" He jumped up to see if he had any bread left in the freezer.

Very few words were spoken over the toast.

"Look. I was just getting ready to go talk to the cops about some stuff. It might be nice if you come along and clear my name, cause....because nothing happened with us. I mean. I don't know how you got that black eye and shit. I dipped." John was laser focused on clearing his name.

"I have a friend who's a cop—"

"You what?"

"Well. I mean I met a detective yesterday, who is helping me to piece together a time-line of sorts."

"I sure hope you told this detective that I didn't do *anything*," attempting to be firm yet easygoing with his tone.

"Look. That's the problem. I don't remember *what I did*— much less what you or anyone else for that matter did— and that's what I told her. I honestly did not want to come here today but I need some answers. You and I were... well...I felt like maybe we coulda been...I kinda remember us on the couch out front."

"Frankie. I wasn't completely honest with you—frankly I have been being kind of a douche bag the past two years— I have a girlfriend back home." He paused so that she could get the message loud and clear. "Yeah. I go out a lot here in Berkeley, and I have my share of fun, but I am always thinking about her...which I know was not fair at all to you. Well. With the coffee dates and all that, I shoulda told you. But it's not like we were dating or some shit. I figured it's just how campus life flows, ya know?"

They looked into each other's eyes at exactly the same time. Beau saw his younger sister, pleading with her pain, driving deep into his gut and far into his subconscious— knowing the right thing to do and the desire to do right— fighting against his insecure self.

Frankie saw a muscle-bound teddy bear, his eyes telling her he cared. While his hands fidgeted and twisted with doubt. How could she turn this around? She needed his help but was really unsure what she was asking of him. Could either of these two find redemption in the other?

A trigger seemed to connect in her mind—dancing with Edgar, drinking from his cup—it dissolved into more of a dream she'd maybe had. Trying to recall a foggy disjointed memory. It fades and then is gone. "I drank too much." Breaking the stare.

"It wasn't just alcohol, Frankie. If you only knew."

"You mean that hip-nowl and GHB?"

Once again they were deep in each other's eyes, this time distrust and anger percolating in.

"How? Where? Who told you? You know about the ruffies?" After a beat, relief shown on his face, *he was not the snitch here.* "Tell me what you heard, or what you felt? Do you remember who gave you a drink after I left that night?"

"I don't remember a thing—but a friend—well a person who found me Friday, gave me a pretty decent description of my being completely out of it. That was Friday. I have only garbled memories of three whole days, Beau. I really, really need to find out what happened."

"So, where'd you get the drug ref?"

"At Tang. I went in to talk to my coach yesterday. I missed practice on Friday and he took me in to get checked out. Then

212

some cop appeared and a nurse had told her about drugs. Well. I…I thought they gave me drugs at Tang cause I was hurt but the nurse started telling me about illegal drugs and asked me to talk to her friend—who was… who is a cop, but she wasn't on duty. I didn't say your name and I didn't want to talk to anyone, but I can't remember anything." The crying was more subdued but started right back up again.

"Wait. So Tang center told you about ruffies? I'm confused. When was this?" Beau felt like he needed to write shit down and grabbed for a notebook. "Sunday. You went to Tang on *Sunday* and they found drugs in your system?"

"I guess so yeah. They said they wanted to ask me where I got some GHB because another girl was in the hospital from Thursday night and—"

"Wait. What other girl? Let's start with Thursday. You and I kinda…well, I dipped at about ten forty-five Thursday. How long did you stay?"

Through tear-filled eyes and shortness of breath. "Beau. I honestly don't remember even what *we* did. It's all garbled together with some dancing…maybe with Edgar Munoz. Do you know him?"

"Holy shit. Wait. What time did you *get* to the barge? Tell me exactly what you can remember. Who were you with and what did you drink?" He'd seen a few episodes of CSI in his day. "Who did you go to the party with, Frankie? Think."

"I went with my curling group. I was with Jane…Jane and Anne and Beth. We were…we Ubered. Oh shit. Lemme check my phone for what time we arrived."

The two spent nearly an hour working out what they believed Thursday night entailed—punch was too large a vehicle to get that much drug into any one person. The red cup she'd held must have been tampered with. At any rate, Frankie had texted Renee about a possible meet up.

"Look, Beau. I don't know why or how much, but I trust her, and her friend Stacey, the nurse. They seemed to know a lot more. Let's talk to her."

"A female detective and you think she's gonna believe me? Nope. Not happening. I am going in on my own."

"Okay, dummy. It's not about just popping in there, you know? Strut up to the station front desk and say I got information. This is not *Cops* on the WB. It's a real case. Renee is way cool—not girly-girly is putting it mildly. Give her a chance."

"Dummy?" They both laughed. It sorta felt like the ice was melting a bit, and this glacial issue was going to manageable after all.

Frankie's phone blinged and she checked the text. "Gypsy's. Dry toast is great and all but I am freakin' craving the alfredo. She'll be there in ten. Let's hit it."

"Don't say hit it, k?" they laughed again. Baby steps.

Edgar

Edgar had been busy in fixer-mode for days. He'd forgotten about a paper due and had zero desire to get outta bed. He was jonesin' for a dose, just a hit of something. Needs to be an upper, 'cause today's another big day.

First day back to practice after all the drama. Facing the guys and hoping above all that the two, Dewey and Beau, who were mentioned in the text that was to be immediately deleted, are none the wiser.

Slippery slope that GroupMe can be. Tell one. Tell all. Tell none—clean-up was certainly not his strong suit. Deny until you die. If no one ratted him out, the story would be a one and done. *Damn where's my secret stash? Shit, right. Flushed it down the toilet when I cleaned out all the bedding and such Friday morning. Gonna have to text the big guy for a bag.*

"QtrPDC." he typed. He needed two fifty in cash and should be able to meet a rep at the player development center study room within an hour.

"kkkc." Three ok's for amount, location and timing, the c for cash only.

As he heaved himself to an upright, he checked his twitter feed—up to the minute soccer scores, shark sightings.

Jessica

Jessica lay flat on her back thinking about what had transpired. Her life was basically over anyways; no need to turn back now.

She'd spent two full days collecting up the meds the nurses gave her, once even having to pop them into her mouth and out again to avoid being caught. She figured she had enough of her mother's valium in her pocketbook to do the trick, if she simply mixed some of this heavy duty shit they doled out.

"Sorry, I can't." was all she could get onto the text to her mother.

I can't swim anymore. I can't marry Nord anymore; he will probably never speak to me again. I can't wear white, well hell, there won't be a wedding to wear white to. I can't face my father. I can't.

I'll never be whole again. I'll never make a good...*anything.*

I won't be hissed about and prodded about and pointed at. Not me. I won't and I can't and I never, ever, ever want to face another day.

She popped the whites, the blues, and two reds for good measure—fight for Stanford red. She began to cry. She was pretty sure the reds were just extra strength cold medicine, but go out on a red. Sleep as soon as possible.

She'd practiced closing her eyes and looking for the white light in her forehead in order to fall right to sleep for years—success—mission accomplished.

216

She was gone within the hour.

Roberta

"I'm very sorry, Mr. Tucker. We did everything we could. We'll know in a day or two what—well, how—the doctor will meet with you in the conference room on two."

Roberta couldn't hold the professionalism one more minute. She scurried to the staff-only restroom.

Dazed and confused, Tuck climbed in the bed with his baby girl and cried out like a hyena for the both of them. His wife had simply refused to even come along with him to the hospital.

Blotto, Frankie & Beau

"So. I have to tell you up front Frankie, I am working today. I realize we are just grabbing a bite to eat, but I have a definite mission to get to the bottom of the incidents from the past seventy-two hours or so, and—"

"No need, Renee, I told him. Save the lectures. We are here to give you information…on the record." She glanced to her left to see Beau's face, which was, of course, focused on the tile floor. *Could she actually trust this guy?*
OhmyGod ohmyGod ohmyGod look up asshole.

"Uh, yeah," mumbling from six inches down.

217

"Good, good, that's outta the way. This place has *the best* chicken parm." *Go easy Renee. Don't spook them.* They were next in line to get the food. *Start 'em eating. Relax.*

"I'll have the chicken parm, and they're on my tab, Gustavo," she said, handing over the plastic credit card.

"Detective." Gustavo nodded back. Renee and her partners were regulars.

"Crazy Alfredo, please," Frankie added.

"Uhm. Meatball calzone. Can you put another meatball on the side? Uhm, wait," he looks timidly to Blotto and gets a nod. "Yeah, meatball on the side, and a Snapple."

"Any other drinks?" Gustavo inquired.

"Just water for me," Frankie adds politely.

"The usual. Uh, make me up a crazy alfredo to go in a bit." Blotto smiles at Frankie. "That's my second favorite. That'll do it, G," the detectives' nickname for Gustavo.

As they grabbed their drinks and popped in a window spot—their eyes met when they realized at the same time —*what if someone sees us?* Too late.

Blotto moved in with a tea and lemonade mix of some kind with. "Hey, my usual table. Nice."

Frankie commented on the weather, Beau turned his chair inwards away from outside eyes, or so he hoped.

"Takes a minute, but food here's worth the wait," observed Blotto.

"Yup. Been here. I love the Calzone but can never finish it." *Cheery. Stay upbeat. Come on, Beau. Just give an inch here buddy.*

About ninety-three seconds later, the glacier of silence became a volcano of words.

"So. You know about the drugs right?" Beau was speaking in an odd speedy Gonzales manner. "And you know that I had nothing to do with anything that happened to Frankie—or that other girl. I already talked to the police and that when I went there I didn't even know about the drugs. Do you need to turn on a tape recorder, or some shit? I mean. Sorry, but this is important that you know I had nothing to do with anything."

"73," their order number came from the loud speaker.
Saved. Thank you, G.

"I'll get it." Blotto was up in a flash.

"I'll help," added Frankie. Right behind her to the counter. *Breathe. Don't cry. Breathe. Why all the fuckin tears these days?*

It was only the Alfredo ready. Frankie was back to the table quick with the hot plate. "I promise. She's cool. Just trust. Well. Let's just eat first."

"Go ahead and eat. The calzone takes longer." Beau was back to speaking to his knees.

The food offered up a solid eight minutes of no need to speak. Renee was eyeballing the two kids and decided to start out easy. "Like I said, best chicken parm. Forgot to ask if either of you wanted a bite."

"I'm good." Full-mouthed.

"I can barely finish my own, thanks though Ren...Detec... what should we call you?"Frankie blushed.

Dewey

Dewey got off the train in Emeryville and texted Beau. "RIDE? AT AMTRAK."

"FTFO." appeared instantly on his screen.

"DUDE. SORRY. DIDN'T KNOW YOU WERE THAT INTO HER."

Yeah he knew all caps pisses some people off but fuckit if he needed autocorrect fucking with him. He switched apps and ordered an Uber.

Once he was in the white Prius he'd ordered up, he flipped to Twitter and Instagram. Lots of shit flying. *Wait. What? 'Female student dead as a result of a night on the Barge.' WTF? OMG. Is it...holy fuck? OMG.*

"Hey uh. Drop me at PDC, will ya?" Dewey mutters to the Uber driver.

"Wasssat...you say Peemount? I go Peemount."

Fuck it. I'll stop by and drop my bag at the house. "Fine. Pee Mount ya MFW."

No way. She couldn't be.Who has the scoop? Wait. Any emails? Fuckin iCloud gives him the "memory almost full" message on the screen. "Fuck Me."

"Hey. You no want wide? I dwop heah?"

"This driver is seriously fucking annoying."

"Wash yo language."

"So *now* you speak English?" Dewey scoffed.

Back to Frankie, Beau, Blotto

Frankie cleared the lunch plates as Renee began to ask Beau for permission to record their conversation from here on out.

"Nothing to hide. Record, write, whatever." He shrugged.

He didn't add much to her case for almost a half an hour of chatter. He said, she was, they were...until a long pause.

"What is it?" Renee could see something was eatin' at this kid. "I can turn off the recorder."

"Cool. Could ya? Just for a sec?" He was a scared little boy inside all that brawn.

When he felt safe that no one could over hear them, he leaned in and pulled Renee and Frankie's shoulders over the table into a

221

huddle. "The drugs, the roofies, the GHB...it's all getting outta hand over there."

"How do you mean, outta hand?" Renee couldn't take notes bent over the table like this.

"Well, basically....I mean....it's like the barge has a shit ton of storage. Well, I don't have 'all access' ya know?"

"All access?" Renee was confused. Frankie completely flabbergasted by his admission to *knowing* about drugs there.

"Like. Some of the guys—well—one guy, is the point man. Like. It's not considered on campus, you know. The thing is..." Beau had seen more than one rat beaten to within inches of his life for crossing the dealer. "I can't say for sure. Well. I think if you talk to Raul."

"Raul. Raul What? Can you let me write this down? You need to be okay with giving me these names, Beau. I can keep your name out of the report but I gotta have something." Renee could feel her heart rate increase. "I don't think you realize how bad off the other victim really is. We need to get to the source. Test the drugs you all are buying...and selling."

"Raul is just a buyer. Raul and Edgar are point on the different stuff. Like. One is pinks, the other blues, ya know?"

"No. I don't know. You need to give me more. Have you got any of the stuff on you? Can you get some? Maybe we set up. Well. Where do they get...hang on..." *Damn I need this kid to come in and make a formal statement.*

"Hey so. I gotta get home to be ready for practice in a few. Mind if I dip out?" saved by the Frankie bell.

"Right. Well listen. I'll give you guys a lift. Beau if you don't mind just coming back to my office after we drop Frankie. We can look at a color chart I got that will help me figure out if its Rohpynol, or whatever..."

"Uh...I..."

"Won't take long at all." Renee was not taking no for an answer. "I'm parked right out front."

"At least it's not a squad car," joked Frankie, trying her best to lighten the mood. "You take shotgun. I'm getting out first." She opened the door for him. *What did I ever see in this lunkhead? Druggie no less. No wonder they always finish second.*

Frankie & the Squad

Frankie arrived at the PDC a bit earlier than Coach expected. *Here goes nothing.* "Hey Coach."

"Oh. Hey...uh, Frankie. Uh, yeah. Come on in. Lan, you got a second? You look good kid. Feeling better?"

AS IF? He set this appointment now playing like he's surprised to see me? And he needs to freaking call for back up? You don't give a flying fuck how I feel, Coach. Unless it affects your salary or points you're always yapping about.

Once the three of them were seated, it became obvious something was up. Silence hung like a pall over the little room as Coach fidgeted with the tchotchke on his desk.

"I needed, well, we needed to talk to you before the squad, Frankie."

"No need, Coach. I brought my gear. I quit." *Don't cry. Breathe. Do not cry.* Water pooled in the lower lids.

"Yeah. Nope. Not gonna happen." *So Landry's now officially in charge of shit? Frankie cannot believe this coach is so freaking weak, man up and say the word rape loser.* Her anger was bringing her a bit of courage.

One lonely salty tear rolled off her cheek and hit her thigh. She shuddered. "Coach, I quit. I'm done."

"Well. Kiddo...it's not that simple."

Fuckin kiddo? Really? Walk out, Frankie. Just stand up and exit the building. Her feet were not listening to her thoughts.

"You know that I have the points system. I can't have you go quitting over this little misunderstanding you had with some boy."

"Look. We don't care if you need to take a coupla days off, but today, this afternoon before practice, you're gonna tell your teammates about what happened to you on
Thursday night."

Obviously, they'd scripted this? Coach must be out of his mind. No fuckin way, bad enough she'd already told him. "If I may borrow your words? Nope. Not gonna happen." Just a sliver of bravery there. *Finally.*

"Aside from what happens to my points, you'd be in jeopardy of losing your scholar—"

"Save it. I quit." *Stand. Fuckin feet, legs move. Let's goooooo. Fuck, fuck, fuck. Do not...* Too late. Tears flowin. *Fuck me.*

"Did you hear? Did you see? Ohmygawd. No way. Yes way. Not that guy? Wait. What? You heard. I heard. She heard, he said, she said."

The group was almost instantly silenced by the trio.

"Ladies. Circle up." Coach was firm, and it was immediately the entire room was at attention mode, eyes on the doorway. Twenty-three girls seated against three inside walls of the room.

Moments earlier, they'd been abuzz and quite chatty over all. Coach wasn't starting practice right at four. They could see the trio talking the past half hour through the glass window of his office, and you-know-what.

A long thirteen seconds later Coach stepped forward into the room. "Frankie has something she'd like to share with you all." He waved his arm towards the doorway, hand pointing to Frankie the way Vanna White turns to the letter board on Wheel.

The tears were now full speed ahead, down, and soaking her tee. Anne jumped up with a Kleenex, and most of the rest of the group's eyes fell to the floor.

Another long silence before Landry stepped into the center of the room to take charge.

"Okay, ladies. You've all been there. Partying it up. One girl voms into her own hair, the other is so wasted you have no idea how she's still standing, the buddy system is the last thing on her mind. Which is why we go over and over and over it in these meetings."

Jane turned a deep purple red and began to cry.

Landry continued, "So. What happens next?"

"I'll tell you what happens." Coach is taking on a big bite, then catches himself.

"This shit happens all the time folks. Which is why I'd like Frankie here to tell you all about how next time you-"

"I'm sorry. I can't. I just can't." Frankie is now being hugged by Anne and Beth in a sort of sandwich-cookie kinda way.

"Okay. So, here's how we're going handle this. Each of you is gonna tell us about that one time—that one thing you did—that well, like...when I was in school, I drank too much and got written up by my RA. Wait. Anyways."

Coach stopped quick and changed direction. "Remember our code of silence? Our team's *can do attitude,* ladies? We are gonna embrace Frankie and talk it out, and keep it amongst

226

ourselves. I *mean* it. Not a word to your parents. Not a peep to your besties or your *DOG for chrissakes*. We will handle this internally."

No one said a word.

"And I have spoken with the Boater assistant coach Carr. We are going to make sure you all are not at the same mixers and athletic sessions for this semester. We'll get through this together. Just like we get through losses, and like we've weathered the fact that we have to travel an hour each way to get ice. This team is the closest I've seen in years, and I know that together you can work this out and be better by Regionals. We have a great outlook this season, and I want you all to take that pledge to work together. No one outside of this room needs to hear or help or offer up fuckin how-to-guides. We know how to win, we are resilient, and this too shall pass." Coach looked from player to player eyeing who he could prod to speak up."

They all stared in disbelief at the Coach. How could he call her out, put her on the spot like this?

"Jane. You've been here a few seasons. You see how we rally and take care of each other, and we'll be better because of days like these, right?"

"Uhm...yeah...sure." Jane looked up briefly but then straight back down to the floor.

"We got a good buddy system and a solid—don't fuck with me on this ladies, our 24 / 48 rule. I am not fucking around this season." Coach paused for affect. "More than likely it was the damned drinking and drugs that got Frankie into this mess if you ask me. No more of this *'golly I could use a second chance'* and shit. That goes especially for you potheads, fucking AD has the random pee tests. I refuse to cover for your asses this time...or send Becky in your place."

A and B almost laughed out loud. The rest of the gang were looking like a bunch of scared kittens. Ninety-eight *pound weakling coach.* Their eyes met with sly grins.

"And I mean it. Not one single one of ya's needs mommy or daddy to tell you how to pull up those big girl panties and get to work. Coach El is in the weight room ready for you all. Let's hit it. Let's go pump some iron." Clapping wildly, as if his fighter were entering the big ring.

Slowly, silently, they made their way out of the locker room. Left behind were Jane and Marla, tending to the dripping tears, assuring their pal 'everything's gonna be okay.'

"Okay, ladies. You too." Landry plopped down next to Frankie and gave the other two the stink eye.

"Frankie. You need to calm down. Collect your thoughts for today, and we'll see you back here tomorrow. Can I help?"

"Thanks, Lan, but I really, really am done. I just can't." With all her might she stood and exited towards the laundry and equipment room.

"Alisson. It's been real." She dropped her loop and the last of her Cal gear on the counter for check-in with Allison the equipment manager and walked out. *Some reason. I feel one helluva lot lighter.*

With each block she walked closer to her apartment, she began to feel better and better. A bit of clarity, a bit of closure. She'd worry about the details later. Of course the coach would be only worried about himself, his point system, his not getting some percentage of a raise If she quit.

Tonight, she'd pop in a rising-crust DiGornio and catch up on Homeland. *I think I can I think I can. Puff puff, chug chug choochoo.* She laughed audibly about her childhood memory.

That lightened mood was not to last.

Renee & Stacey

Stacey and Renee were at odds about how to handle the news. Mainly, who was going to tell Frankie, and when.

"She hears a rumor or sees it on the news and she might just bust up inta a million tiny pieces," Stacey lobbied.

"Look. I dunno what to tell ya on this one, Stace. The girl just poured her whole heart out. She is feeling a bit better just because that fucker confessed that he's a true douchebag. It was almost like his approval was all she was craving. Little fucker. You bring up the gang bang theory or the Stanford girl to her today and *poof,* there goes my best witness."

"Seriously? You're gonna bring up another fucking case at a time like this? Think Renee, think. This girl hears the other one offed herself and we got way bigger problems than your freaking drug case. I, for one, will not stand by and let this kid crumble right before my...our eyes. You with me, or not?"

Stacey held the door open daring her to stay put on the big comfy couch.

It was five o'clock traffic no less, but they were doing what they had to do. "Lemme just pop into my place to get outta this monkey suit." Renee was sweating profusely, though the outside temp was a mild seventy-two.

"Fine." Stacey was busying herself on the iPad with googling "what not to say" and "survivor's resources in the bay area."

Frankie

Frankie set the oven temp to 425 and cued up Netflix. She was teary a bit ago when she realized she'd forgotten to take the 'stool softener' and solid food was maybe gonna make her need to shit before too much longer. *When was the last time I fuckin pooped?*

Homeland is so fuckin fake. If I'd hair and make-up who says I can't be the next Claire D?

Was that a knock at the door, or was it on the show?

Oven mitts on, she ignored the first wraps. She heard the next ones as far too loud, for friendly. As she turned to the sound, the oven door slammed startling her from behind while her heart raced in the front. "Who's there?"

Pep talking herself. *Sound sorta chill, Renee.* "Just us, Frankie."

Us? Sounds familiar but can't quite place it. "Gimme a sec." *Think. Think. Think. Maybe just another word or two I'll recognize the voice.* "Are you in a hurry?" Heart pounding in her throat. Who drops by unannounced? If it's someone from the team.

"Nah kid. Just here for a quick. Well to say hi, and—"

"Oh hey, Stacey. Are you checking up on me, already?" She pulled the door open with a smile. "Hey, Renee. Wassup?" *Two on one, but they couldn't possibly know about the team scene.* "I just threw in a pizza. Come on in." *Their smiles seem really fake.*

Awkward silences were dangling on a regular basis these days. Neither Renee nor Stacey took steps forward into the apartment right away.

"Uh. Yeah. Well. We can't stay, but..." suddenly Renee was the bumbling idiot with her words.

Stacey fake punched her in the arm. "We can stay a minute, no hurry, just....like you say...checking up on ya." Her eyes not directly making contact with Frankie's causing suspicion.

"Uhhh." *What the fuck is it now? I got aids from this shit? Damn they both look ghastly.* "Well. Come in. Take a load off." *There's that black cloud feeling again. Fuck. Fuck. Fuck. Do not cry.* Tear ducts filling up without warning.

"Oh, Frankie." Stacey began crying, and hugging her and suffocating her. Renee with the longest arms made it a family sandwich.

After a moment, they broke free and simply stood as if they were circling a dead bird. All three subdued and looking at the floor.

Renee grabbed Stacey's hand ever so slightly. "Let's sit down." No formal living area or couch so they parked on stools at the kitchenette.

"Just say it." Through tears. "What have I got? Hepatitis? Aids? *Honestly. What could be more wicked than the last few days?* "Oh gawd. I'm pregnant?" Tears streaming freely now. "Please. Tell me I am not—"

"No. No. No. Frankie. It's not you." Stacey more composed but still unsteady. "We. It's just that. Well—" Stacey abruptly stopped speaking when Frankie turned away and got up.

Frankie opened the fridge. Only one coke. Newman's Own Lemonade carton in the back but from so long ago there was mold forming at the top seam. "Water anyone?"

She shifted to the cupboard and saw a few relatively clean cups stacked from the Giants game last year. Separating them took a bit of pull. She kept her back to the women so as not to call attention to the fact that they may or may not have been washed prior to stacking.

Without a word, she filled three from the tap and set them in the center of the bench which served as a dining space.

No one was thirsty. After another short pause.

"Did you set the timer on your Za?" Renee could hear her own 'fakeness' and shrugged apologetically towards Stacey.

"Listen kid. It's not you. We came over to, well there's been a bit of a…." *Damn. This is tougher than I had anticipated.* "Remember how I told you that the girl from Stanford was in the hospital?"

"Oh God. The dress. How much did it cost? They're suing me for damages now, right?" Frankie's mind was racing. *Couldenta been H&M or Forever 21 fashionista? Fuckin D&G, probably a thousand bucks? Fuckin' rich snobs.* "Dry cleaning won't cut it?"

"No Frankie. It's not the dress. To be honest, I didn't even turn it in yet, and the issue hasn't even come up." Renee was getting some of her old case-worker tone back. "She's dead, Frankie." *Smooth move exlax. Just spit it right out there whydontcha?*

Frankie dropped to her knees on the linoleum. Stacey gave Renee a foul stare then dropped too. It was a most awkward embrace and then blood-curdling sobs. "I'm gonna die?"

The duo managed to get Frankie to her bedroom and calmed down a bit as they explained what had happened. "This person was not nearly as strong as you. Likely had other mental health issues; fear self-magnifies, intensity only as strong as you let it be. A tiny flicker of angst can easily develop into terror in some people. Don't be afraid. Talk it out. The energy it takes to grow fear into a dangerous level." Frankie heard none of it.

233

She's dead. I coulda died. I still could die.This is never going to go away.

"Talk it out. Confront the fears head on. Don't let this incident paralyze you into inaction. In reality, shit never lives up to the negative disaster that plays out in our minds." The smoke alarm went off in the other room. They'd completely charred the DiGiorno.

Once the ruckus of the smoke alarm was dealt with, the trio huddled up on the floor in Frankie's bedroom.

"I am so ashamed. It's like being a girl people expect you to act a certain way. Then if a coach expects something entirely different, there's that stress. I just don't want to deal. I hear the way people are talking about me."

"Let them gossip, kid, you know you."

"Yeah, I know me. The slut, the whore, the druggie. It's like I never even—"

"Wait right there. You are not any of those things, Frankie. You know my story. You think I am a slut or a whore?" Stacey was eye-to-eye daring her.

"You're different. You're older and you—"

"I was nineteen, kid. A year younger than you. Today, I sit on this floor in this shit bag of an apartment—no offense —and I am right back in my own skin reliving the nightmare of that *exact* day. Days...months...years of selfdeprecating and self-shaming." An authenticity in her voice. "I am only me, kid. One fucked up,

234

baggage-ridden, greasy-grimy me. I have spent so many years in my own private hell. Let me be there for you, with you. Let Renee put these fuckers away for the drugs and abuse. It's the only way to endure, persevere, relieve, or support the next victim. We can, and we must do more to make change. I need you, kid. Can't you see what you have done for me in the last few days? You've unlocked the hellhole prison of my own shame."

"She's right, kid. I've known Stace practically my whole life and I gotta say, this shit is real. I love her like a sister.
She never once let on why or what made her icy and indifferent around men. She ain't a lesbian like me, but she sure can serve up a mad stink-eye to dick barflies. Pardon my French but she's a real bitch on wheels some days."

"Uhm, golly. Thanks, pardner—you're the bitch. But that's beside the point. We want to do this right, kid. We need you. You need you. For all the shit they teach you in school or sports, they never ever give you a lesson on how to lose—well cope—you know, fucking survive overwhelmingly bullshitty shit."

"Bullshitty?" they all broke into laughter.

It's another half hour before they determine the growling in their stomachs must be dealt with.

"Chinese? There's a place way up on Shattuck where it's so dark you can barely see your food, much less any campus-gawkin-freak-talkers."

Stacey really does seem different, possibly even younger today.
"Fine. Lemme get my UGGS and a sweatshirt. This place is fucking

235

freezing after dark." Admittedly, she was not quite ready to be alone with her thoughts on this just yet.

As they hit the stairs down to jump in the car, they spotted Holly strolling the sidewalk. "Hey. Just sorta walking by."

"Walking by, eh?" Frankie is not fooled. "Let's go, little miss noblewoman. We are getting Chinese."

It's a silent ride to the restaurant but after getting seated in a circle booth, the conversation flows over favorite dishes, best ever fortunes, water chestnuts not being watery, who eats duck feet? A genuinely decent banter amongst the foursome and welcome deviation from the elephant in the backs of all their minds.

Renee orders green tea ice cream for the entire bunch, shocked that not a one of them has ever ventured to try it. "I'm buying. So don't get your panties in a wad about the tab. Who wants coffee?"

"Coffee, at this hour? You're such a cop, Renee." True merriment amongst the group.

Until that first tear. *This is fuckin insane. She's dead. I'm laughing about Chinese ducks with three complete fuckin strangers. Fucking tear ducts are freakin' drivin' me crazy. Who am I? I want my life back. I wanna go home...I can't go home. I'll never be able to face my family—they're gonna know —everyone knows. I just wanna. Dammit.*

"Okay, kid. Let it out. We can. Well, damn. I ain't gonna *make* you eat the shit." Renee trying a bit of humor to lighten the moment.

"I'm sorry," interjects Holly. "I probably should not have come. You guys—"

"You're sorry? Fuck that. You—" Frankie began.

"Okay, gang. Let's lighten up." *Careful Stacey.* "Holly. We are delighted to have you join us, and, Frankie, we gotta slow down on the F word out in—"

"Fuck, fuck, fuck, fucking fuck." shouted Frankie, just as the waitress arrived with the tray of green globs. "Uh, sorry." She straightened her posture ever-so-slightly and wiped her mouth with a napkin.

The table sat silently as a small bowl was placed in front of each of them. Just fourteen seconds later Frankie broke into laughter. "Well. Fuck me," she whispered under her breath. Another giggle-fest—shorter this time, as Stacey decided it was time.

"Holly. I need a favor."

"Yeah, sure, anything."

"We. Uh. Well. When we came by earlier. Golly, how do I say this?" Stacey stuttered.

"The fucking Stanford girl *died,* Holly. She *died*. She's *dead*."

Frankie was ranting but in a bit softer voice, and nearly dry eyes. "Dead. Can you fuckin believe it? I coulda died. I think you probably saved me and shit. Fucking died."

"Let's not get ahead of ourselves here."

Holly was wide-eyed and took a minute to process the information.

"Dead? But how? From what? Why?" Holly choked back tears. "Did you know her too?" She turned and addressed Renee and Stacey. "Wait. Are you sure?"

No one spoke for a second, just nods. Frankie got up. "I gotta pee." All eyes on her. She turned back to the table. "Just gonna pee for fuck's sake. Not off myself."

"Oh my God." Holly's tears flowed.

While she was away from the table, Stacey explained to Holly how fragile the situation was. How Frankie had the hard outer shell but might need a friend to stay the night. Explaining as quickly as she could, how they had found out. What the doctors suspected—rumors—not in the news but soon.

"So. Renee and I go way back, as you can see," she said, when Frankie was back within ear shot. "Hard friends are good to come by," she said with a grin.

"Not that funny Stace," Renee added. "You okay, kid? Ready to roll?"

"Okay? There is no such thing, detective. But, yes, let's get outta here."

Frankie had composed herself as best she could; splashed cold water on her swollen eyes, and was feeling pretty tired all of a sudden. "I need Netflix and my pillow, el wrapeedoe."

"Thanks for dinner. And. Well, thanks," Frankie said, as she climbed outta the Prius.

"Holly. Can we drop you at your place?" inquired Renee.

"Mind if I stay for some Netflix, Frankie? I don't have it at my place."

"Fine." Frankie rolled her eyes and shut the door before Stacey could offer up a hug or some other gesture that might start the tears again.

"Well, that was unbelievably awful. Drinks?"

"I'm buying." Blotto pulled into the Safeway lot on College. Both got out and headed into the grocery. As they rounded the aisle for liquor a few college boys were discussing volume and alcohol content best bang for a buck. They continued past to the Mike's Hard Lemonade and checked out in silence. Not until they reached Renee's place did Stacey speak. "It's not over for Frankie you know."

"Hell. I am more worried about you, Stace. It's not over for any of us."

THE END.

GLOSSARY

A

F As Fuck. Translation: the horror film was scary AF (as fuck)!

Betches Friends or pals – usually female.

BFW Be. Fucking. Ware. Translation: there is trouble brewing, beware, say nothing, admit nothing. If coach or admin asks for definition: Big Fucking Whoop.

CMB Call me back.

CMM Call me maybe. Translation: it's casual, call me back if or when you want to.

DDD Deny Deny Deny. Translation: dude duck down, someone knows something. If coach or adult asks for definition: Doing Did Done.

EROC End Rape On Campus. Legitimate organization helping victims and survivors. www.eroc.org

FBO Face Book Official. Translation: *usually* both parties agree to be in some sort of relationship.

FML Fuck My Life. Translation: someone maybe has a pimple, or has had bad news of some kind causing them to dramatize their sentence with FML.

IFC Interfraternity Council. Most universities with Greek houses have these.

IRL In real life. Not certain this term appears in the story, but much of its content is IRL.

LBD Little Black Dress

LOL Lay Low. Translation: Stay out of sight, do not let a coach or administrator get at ya! If anyone asks for definition, just begin laughing.

MCGC Multi-Cultural Greek Council

PDC Player Development Center. Translation: lockers, weights, equipment, training, study rooms – all exclusively for athletes only.

POI Person of Interest – police matter

RTFM Read The Freaking Manual (sometimes a less polite term is used in place of "Freaking")

GHB or Ruffies Date rape drugs. Translation: some of what Bill Cosby made popular in the news

WTF Why the frown. Translation: what the fuck were you/was I thinking.

YOLO You only live once.

GROUP DISCUSSION QUESTIONS

1. How did you experience the book? Were you engaged right away or did it take a while?

2. How did you feel reading it – annoyed by the style? Sad, bored, disturbed, confused?

3. One early edition reader did not think it was believable that Jane would leave Frankie alone at the party, though it can, does, and did happen. Can you recall a similar situation?

4. Did the book change your opinion about any recent news stories you may have heard or read about on the topic of hazing, underage drinking, or young adult suicide?

5. Do you feel different about any of the above topics after having read it?

6. Was there a character in the book that you connected with, or could relate to, from your college days?

7. What feelings did this book evoke for you?

8. What do you think the author's purpose was in writing this book? What ideas was he or she trying to get across?

9. Does the fact that it is based on true events surprise you?

ACKNOWLEDGMENTS

I had quite a bit of support in getting this first draft to a point where I felt it was ready for share. Thank you all!

It is not tidy, professionally edited, or literary genius. It is my attempt to do a little something in effort to call for change – on the topics of hazing, University cover ups, and #metoo. Not much has changed in the past 20+ years, the time to speak up is now.

It has meant a lot to me to have early readers agree there is a need for a story like this one to open dialogue among young people. A suggestion made by most readers over age 40 is to start with the GLOSSARY so that you aren't annoyed by the DDD or LOL.

It is necessary for me to say that I do not expect readers to find this well polished, edited, or written. It simply is what it is, and I believed important enough to self-publish.

Please share and help avoid another SHE TOO. Thanks, in advance, Rhonda

67780280R00152

Made in the USA
Columbia, SC
01 August 2019